But that's absurd

But that's absurd

A
tall story
without
that most common
fifth sign of our abc

Gordon John Harrison

authorHOUSE®

AuthorHouse™
1663 Liberty Drive
Bloomington, IN 47403
www.authorhouse.com
Phone: 1-800-839-8640

First published by AuthorHouse   12/23/2011

ISBN: 978-1-4567-8065-4 (sc)
ISBN: 978-1-4567-8066-1 (ebk)

Printed in the United States of America

I

It was a bright cold day in April and my clock was striking thirty six. Sounds familiar? All right, I do admit that this is hardly an original start to this curious story which I am about to commit to writing. But as anybody so foolish as to carry on absorbing this particular opus will find out, I am no wordsmith. This is in fact my first foray into that difficult world of writing a book. I was always told that apart from having an involving plot and a convincing cast to attract and maintain its public, a good yarn has to draw bookworms in, right from its first group of words. So hats off to that famous British author of *Animal Farm* for providing inspiration for my introduction.

In fact it was in April and it was bright and cold but my alarm clock was actually ringing at six thirty a.m. as this saga burst in upon my normally placid humdrum disposition. At that waking hour on that particular morning, I was making my usual first contact with my twin across in my bathroom mirror and bidding him good day. But I found out to my horror that I could not talk lucidly. I was virtually dumb. Trying hard, a word or two did blurt out from my mouth but abruptly I could not say a thing. Stop . . . start . . . stop . . . start. Paralysis.

I was hoping it would pass. For almost half an hour I sat at my dining room window, calling out to my cat Monty, to jump in and savour a morning dish of fish I had for him—but to no avail. I could only murmur a passing noun or an occasional consonant—and all I got for my charity was a curious look and a snub from that unthankful animal. Why or how had I lost my normal vocal capability? In fact, it was all stupid. I had no cough nor cold. I did not pass away any twilight hours of last night shouting loudly at a football match nor arguing, as is my want, about politics with that stubborn right-wing MP living two doors away. In fact from noon to night, it was just yours truly, calm and happy with my own company, living solo in my flat, doing nothing as usual but absorbing a titillating book, with a soothing CD of Mozart playing on my hi-fi. But now, in this cold light of day, I was mostly taciturn, stopping and starting to talk to my shadow, occasionally finding I could put across small groups of words, such as "Talk, you fool!" "Shout out loud!" "This is ridiculous!"

In truth, what a good job it was that today was a Saturday. So I had a day or two in hand to sort out my vocal chords again prior to turning up for my job this coming Monday night, waiting on patrons at Luigi's Trattoria in Farringdon, North London.

An action plan was vital. To start with, I just had to go out of my flat, visit local shops and try various forms of communication with normal humans, or I would go crazy. So a quick jump into my trusty old Ford Focus and I was off with alacrity to stock up my cupboard with provisions. This outing was crucial as Lisa, my loving but pugnacious bosom pal, was aiming to turn up tonight following a four month trip abroad. My plan was to cook a tantalising dish or two and, with luck, to catch up on a long hot night of passion. This was not surprising as I was waiting faithfully, abstaining monastically from any amorous activity.

But to bring my long drawn out chastity to a halt, it was obviously crucial that I should talk and act normally again with Lisa. So I thought I would not pay a visit as usual to our local Sainsbury's, but would call at a small community shop in our town, which is run by my wily long standing Indian chum, Sanjay Kapur. This kind old chap was always happy to say a warm "good morning" and to chat for hours. And I had to try to chat. For hours if I had to.

In my hand I had my usual list of organic products and low fat brands and as always, to bring it all back, a quantity of plastic shopping bags as my contribution to saving our world from a gigantic mountain of rubbish.

"Why if it isn't my buddy, Paul. How you doing?"

"V . . . v . . . w . . . thanks". Such was my pitiful partial outburst.

Sanjay put on a curious look.

"You OK, old son? Too much boozing last night, no?"

"No. I just can't sp . . ." I got thus far and basta, couldn't finish. Why did I stop half way through in this way?

Sanjay had to laugh. "Lost your vocals, old chum. Struck dumb?"

I ran my hand across my lips with a vacant shrug.

"You talk too much, no? Not to worry. Just go round my gondolas and pick out what food and drink you want."

I was happy simply to shop and stay schtum but automatically said out loud: "Thanks a lot, Sanjay"

My pal was aghast—and so was I. "Paul. That's you talking. Back to normal now? You just said 'Thanks a lot'."

"That's right, I did say 'thanks a lot'". I was dumbstruck too. Valid words from my mouth. Was I in fact lucid again?

"Fantastic!" said our Indian buddy. "So your block is not continuous. O.K. Just carry on trying to talk or it could all vanish again". But my mind was a blank and stupidly I did not know what to say.

I got a prompt from Sanjay. "In fact, how about you trying to say . . . umm . . . 'Vindaloo curry with poppadums'".

"Vindaloo curry with poppadums"

"Amazing! I'm hungry just by your saying it. Now try 'Two Birijani and a Rogan Josh'"

"Two Birijani and a Rogan Josh—wow! I did it". I was blissfully happy.

"You know, you ought to do a waiting job in an Indian joint, not a high flown Italian dump" said Sanjay with a mocking look. "A last go. Say 'two Goodhi Bhaji and a Khat Mithi Gobi'. It's a tasty mouthful, but can you talk about it?"

I said it with no stumbling. Sanjay's grin was gigantic. "You got it now. It sounds all back to normal. So how about simply saying out loud all that's put down on your shopping list?"

"Br . . . B . . . T . . ." Catastrophic! I could not murmur a word from that list. I was back to my block. I had to admit that my affliction was again virtually total.

Sanjay was full of sympathy, watching as I slowly did my shopping, stomping up and down his rows of goods with a look that could kill, picking out provisions from his tidy displays of tins and packs, angry at my idiotic actions, or should I say inactions. As I was finally paying, Sanjay, with a kindly look, said "Paul, old son, if I was you, if you want to talk again, I should stop buying British food and go totally Indian—that way you won't go hungry. Or if not, just rush out and consult a good doctor straightaway."

I was still in a painfully black mood on arriving back at my flat, and had to admit that Sanjay was right. I should talk as soon as I could to a doctor—and not just any ordinary quack. Doing a bit of googling on my PC, I found a psychiatrist with a diploma in what is known as 'aphonic obtrusion', who was, surprisingly, working on Saturdays and Sundays. So I rang him and was put through to his assistant. But could I talk? Miraculously on this occasion, I said all my words without a hiccup.

"May I book a consultation with Doctor Mark Smith, now, today, or tonight? My situation is critical."

"Sorry, sir. Doctor Smith is unusually busy today and has no vacancy at all".

It was probably on account of my loud groan that his assistant was so obliging.

"But Doctor Smith has a gap at two o'clock tomorrow, Sunday, if that suits you. But at his consultancy in Slough"

"Thanks a lot. Do book it, if you would".

"To whom am I talking?"

"Paul Morrison"

"Thank you, sir. Till tomorrow."

But I was not totally out of harm's way. I had to think how, in my disastrous condition, I should plan my catch up with Lisa. As I think I told you, Lisa is a darling but can turn into a distinctly bloody mood if things do not work out right. Calamity was looming. How will things pan out for us if I can only say occasional words or—horrors—if I am totally dumb? With so much to impart. To say nothing of a bit of nocturnal fun on my divan. It could all wind up catastrophically, I know.

Now wait an instant! I just had a crazy thought. If I find I cannot actually talk, I can always say things in writing, can't I? Brilliant! Hastily I took out a thick crayon and a pad and found that nothing could stop my scribbling any old word or thought. "Hi Lisa, you look stunning!" was my first try. Good looking writing too. Lisa will laugh and join in this fun. Now I had to start to tidy up all this chaos so that my flat was looking warm and romantic.

Two hours' hard work, scrubbing, dusting and sorting, a quick whip round with my Dyson®—with my poor cat thrown out—and it was all Bristol fashion. I was just following my list of do's and don'ts. Lots of voluptuous pink tulips, Lisa's colour. O.K. Soft lights, cool! Also, though I am loath to admit it, a dusty vinyl disc of Frank Sinatra crooning away as background. Sinatra! Good Lord! So old hat, but Lisa actually finds him cuddly! And also Ray Conniff. Foot tapping rubbish to my mind, but that also turns our lady on. Anybody would think Lisa was fifty, not around half that tally. Talk about dumbing down! I find that sort of music humdrum and monotonous. If it was my call, I would favour as background a compilation from my stock of sultry Brazilian samba music—Santana, Gal Costa, Antonio Carlos Jobim and company. (That always brought back thoughts of a wild musical holiday in Rio!)

But to adapt a famous saying, "what Lisa wants, Lisa obtains". Anything to put my darling into a cuddly mood. Now all my sitting room had my stamp of approval. So why not pour a big splash of cool Spanish fino as company to savour in my cosy armchair until that classy lady turns up?

I thought Lisa might show up punctually on this occasion, but no. Typically, my paramour was half an hour adrift. Storming in, without apologising, Lisa was a flurry of passion. A big hug and a good strong kiss and an "Awful traffic, darling. So long away. I had a fabulous trip. But I did miss you. And I'm simply starving!"

So it was straight into my dining room for both of us to savour my gastronomic workmanship. Our rapport was still warm and promising. My ladyship said gracious things about my cooking and was a champion of small talk, monopolising our catch up chat totally, I am glad to say. Having put paid to my coconut and banana pudding, my paramour was in a hurry to start launching into a painstaking run through a stack of albums containing probably thousands of colour photos of that safari.

With both of us comfortably on my sofa following a most satisfying long hot kiss, and with a glass of bubbly cava in our hands to toast our union, Lisa had sunk into a long soliloquy about that fascinating trip. Luckily I had not had to say much up to this point and Lisa was not finding anything wrong with my short guttural sounds. I just had to show I was following my *inamorata's* flow of words rapturously.

During that first hour or so, staying dumb did not turn out too much of a quandary, as Lisa had such a gigantic amount to impart. And you can count on it: Lisa could not stop talking about it all lavishly in glowing colour. My option was not to say a word, just nod and grin and murmur odd sounds and allow my amour to carry on and on and on.

Lisa's tour was both a fascinating and important activity—a multi-country fact-finding circuit to look into any migratory habits of birds, taking in Poland, Russia and Scandinavia, tramping through that tundra in Norway, staying in an ornithological control foundation in Oslo and visiting a world famous bird-watching station in Ninji Novgorod. Lisa had had a mania for providing a running account by mailing postcards for my information almost daily from such faraway locations. So I was *au fait* with most of that group's work plan. But now I was to absorb it all again.

"Look, Paul, at this shot. It shows that gigantic automatic Arctic station north of Mount Pallas. It's on a big fiord with a rocky promontory swarming with thousands of common ducks and swans . . . I did an ongoing analysis of major migratory paths" . . .

"Uh-huh", was my only word.

"In this stunning panorama of wild woodland, can you pick out, just by that cliff, that mass of blackbirds, which had no doubt flown in from Scotland? And this too, a shot of lapwings and hawks, gliding across brown swamps. Such a mind-blowing sight in that magic fairy-light Finnish midnight sky . . ."

"Uh-huh".

"Now, Paul, just study this map of our routing. It shows our tour of ornithological staging posts going up into an historic Jurassic strand, not far from Narvik, or was it Tromsö? I can't think for now. Cliffs and crags and rocks, and lots of trips by kayak . . ."

"Uh-huh".

An hour and a half had slid by and I was now looking at photo four four six. Lisa, pausing an instant, took a sip of my bubbly, only to plough on with passion. Talking of which, although I was not about to say anything or in fact could say anything, Lisa's body was truly starting to wind up my libido. That *parfum* Christian Dior, that fragrant skin, that silky hair, that cosy look was frankly totally distracting. Coasting along through that long narration without any physical satisfaction, I found it difficult to stay in control. But Lisa was galloping on.

"Look now. This shot has various unusual migrating birds for this part of Lapland which our group was studying via orthodromic sun compass routing from Canada."

"Uh-huh". (Thinks: "What's that all about?" Thinks again: "What intoxicating pupils Lisa has.")

"Now this group of photos shows all my chums, thirty in all, at a wild birthday cookout for our boss in Kirovsk. All of us had a jolly multi-national singsong. And that all-night frolic our crowd had in a community sauna with that chilly Arctic air full of a spicy odour of burning fir logs—that was a big laugh—so much fun!"

"Uh-huh" (Thinks: "Much fun? What sort of fun?? Hands off, rampant dingos! You all making hay as I stay put, waiting faithfully, abstaining from any amorous activity. Although I do admit that young blond North Country lass living in that stylish barn up our road has got my libido working hard on many an occasion . . .)

Lisa was still in full flight. "How about this for a snap? A bunch of storks drifting across a bright crimson morning sky in that Gulf of Bothnia".

"Uh-huh". I was falling into a stupor, having by now run through fifty additional snowy panoramas. But Lisa was running on, tooth and nail.

"This shot too is outstanding, don't you think? It was in woodland not far from Uppsala, a cuddly group of Parus Montanus—also known as willow tits".

Good Lord, what was that about tits? I was conscious straight away of a stirring in my stomach and a longing for substantial physical contact. That occasional sight of Lisa's light pink orbs moving voluptuously within that stylish stripy shirt was a catalyst for action. As subtly as I could and moving up on my sofa, with my hydraulics starting to spring into motion, my hand just had to start stroking Lisa's thigh. A flush of irritation instantly lit up Lisa's brow.

"Hands off! Not now! It looks as if you don't want to finish this book of my photos? Is it all so frightfully boring, or shall I carry on?"

"Uh-huh!" I said, stopping in my tracks in a bit of a panic.

"And why do you carry on just saying 'Uh-huh'? From my arrival, all you only do is go on blurting out 'Uh-huh'. A brilliant show of non-communication, I must say. Uh-huh! No loving words or a pat on my back. Is all my hard work with difficult photography to obtain such fantastic visuals simply a load of rubbish to you? Is it?"

I was in panic now. I had to try to talk.

"No. Sorry" (Gosh! I got that out.) "Pl . . ." Now my block was back. "I am v . . ." "Pro . . ." "B . . ." My situation was catastrophic. Lisa had put on a mightily angry look. But I thought straightaway about my fallback plan of writing out words to hold up and put across what I had to say but could not. In an instant, I took out a blank scrap of A4 and a thick black crayon from my artist's kit on my work station and in a mad fit of scribbling sought to print out an apology in big bold capitals. Saying sorry for acting so oddly, and announcing that, without knowing why, I had lost my ability to talk normally. Mouthing odd words was all I could do. Holding up my script, I sought Lisa's compassion.

But Lisa, lacking any sign of sympathy, was by now furious. That lady was not for calming or convincing . . . that lady was for burning. Snatching that dismal scrap of graphic information out of my hands and ripping it into tiny bits, my unloving paramour stood up to shout a flow of angry parting words:

"Look Paul, what *is* this crazy story? It sounds absurd and without a word of truth. In fact, for you and I, that's it!

It's curtains . . . all kaput. If that sort of fooling around is all you think of yours truly and my work, frankly you can go and do a funny run. It was good to know you, Paul. Adios." And with that, I saw Lisa, dramatically as always, pick up photos, coat and all, and storm out in a flourish, slamming my front door shut.

So much for a cosy night of intimacy. What a fool I was. But how can you possibly obtain what you fancy from a voluptuous spunky lady if you cannot chat up with loving words but only act dumb? A disastrous assignation. In fact, my only consolation for failing so totally was to call in my faithful Monty from his unkind ostracism out of doors and sinking into my armchair, to sit him comfortably on my lap, stroking him lovingly. In addition, to fill a gigantic glass right up with top quality VSOP cognac and to switch on my TV, slip in a DVD of Dad's Army and Monty Python and chill out, as youth would say. Drowning my sorrows thus, I sank into oblivion.

II

"Ouch! Good morning, daylight. No thanks, that's much too bright!"

Not surprisingly, I slid gradually into a conscious condition that following day with a crucifying throbbing pain in my brain. Burying my brow right down into my pillow and wishing to shut out all that light and all that noisy commotion coming up through my window from my road, I slowly took stock of my situation:

Lisa? Big walkout. What a clumsy unromantic idiot I am! It was all my fault. Attracting that lady back now—a most doubtful proposition. Action plan—a top priority. And my ability to talk? How now brown cow? Just as disastrous as last night. A word or two, and a block to follow. In fact I still cannot say much at all.

Doctor? Ah, that's right, I must look sharp and go through with that consultation, though I doubt if this particular quack will put his digit on any miraculous solution.

Job? Trauma looming in that Trattoria. A critical situation if I cannot talk. I must find a solution during today or on arriving at work tomorrow night, I will look a total fool and probably obtain ignominious dismissal from my angry boss. Curtains to my job and my pay. Financial crisis. Bankruptcy. Doom.

But following an hour of motivation and mobilisation on my part including a long soak in an icy cold bath, I was just about fit to sally forth for my contact with Doctor Mark Smith. His consulting room in Slough was a fair jaunt away. As I did not fancy ploughing out of town through all that M4 traffic in my not too trustworthy motor, my plan was to catch a local train at Paddington station for that half hour trip.

Not having had any inclination to fill my stomach with food prior to going out, I bought two juicy bananas and an organic ham and salad sandwich from a station stall to munch away as I was consulting an indicator board to look for my train. And I quickly saw to my horror that a train to Slough would go off in an instant. Choking on my butty, I ran to Platform 6 as if I was crazy, arriving at its first coach, just as its pair of sliding doors was slowly closing.

A frantic jump and I was aboard, only to find to my dismay that this part of my train was totally full—in fact brimming not just with ordinary folk but with a most amazing throng of humanity from all around our world. This was God country. Sitting or standing and all staring my way without saying a word was a colourful crowd of spiritual officials and principals from all known faiths and cults—Christian (Catholic, Anglican, Apostolic, Baptist, Calvinist and Orthodox), Muslim, Brahmin and Buddhist. Also rabbis from Judaism—in fact all our world's sanctimony, crowding into a small railway wagon. Was I hallucinating? In fact, no. I was just standing foolishly, facing this highly colourful panorama of ministry, with my mouth full of sandwich and with a pair of bananas in my hands. Almost as if I was carrying out a hold-up.

So I stood still, facing this myriad of looks from an array of pairs of black, brown, dark and light pupils, a still wall of ocular curiosity, all trying to work out, without making a sound, who I was, why I was on board and if I was a risk or hazard. Slowly a bald old monk stood up and coming forward, said in a warm and convivial way:

"Hi pilgrim! Your arrival with us all is good, a gift of God. Taking this train can bring to you total salvation, if that is your aspiration. From all lands and towns around this world, our aim in this group, in fact our worldly task, is saving souls. To gain a pardon for all your sins, you must from now on succumb to Almighty God. Join in with us. Fighting against sin is a just war—our only war."

Oh crumbs! I thought. This nutty bunch wants to chat. If I had a wish or in fact a capability to say anything, I probably would blurt out a thing or two but just now, it was an impossibility. Masticating rapidly to swallow my snack and nodding furiously, I was patting my lips, as if to say "can't talk".

But that onslaught from all and sundry around was continuing. A hairy Sikh cut in: "It's all about total truth, pilgrim. Join us. You can follow any faith, you can bow to any God. Christ or Allah or natural spirits. Just admit your sins, promising to talk and act in a virtuous way always and you will know comfort and glory and immortality in unison with us all".

With this probing inquiry continuing, I was starting to worry, as although I had almost nothing in my mouth by now, my vocal chords could hardly function to ask what was going on.

Soon a small crowd of fashion-conscious cardinals and bishops, just back from Vatican City and a Papal symposium, all in sharply cut brown cassocks from a smart Roman tailor and humming a Magnificat, was moving slowly forward. This group took things in hand by satisfying my curiosity and outlining such aims and plans as had this hybrid group of holy mankind (and womankind).

"You will no doubt wish to know all about our organisation and our goals. It is our World Faith Symposium, two thousand participants in all, coming from around our world to that holy city of Swindon for four days of instruction, discussion and production of an action plan for a joyous pacific world. No conflicts, no wars. Faith has no want of arms to win against sin. To whom do all of us pray, you may ask? Through a myriad of ways to a common Almighty, up in that vast starry sky, who is our Holy Saviour, who stands for all, and who absorbs around Him in comfort and joy all spiritual dogmas and convictions."

A tall African Monsignor, swinging his rosary around his thumb and looking straight my way, cut in: "And may I ask which faith do you follow, pilgrim?"

I was now right in a spotlight with that mass of humanity, all staring my way. So I did my utmost to say a word or two—but as usual I would only say odd consonants.

"I don't b . . ." was my total contribution. All around, I saw looks of fascination and stupor.

"I think I know why this man of no words cannot talk." said a rotund bald Scottish Catholic provost, pushing forward. "This lost soul is from a group of ours which avoids talking as part of its philosophy and its way of worship. In fact this good man in our midst is without doubt a Trappist monk, in mufti today, out and about in our world, and so not in his usual monastic habit. Trappists vow to stay dumb and constantly look for union with God, not vocally but spiritually. That holy community has a thirst for mysticism in a sanctuary of total calm. Companionship without sound, in fact, is that flock's motto. A Trappist's words of joy and worship stay in his mind and soul and do not pass into his mouth. Bravo, pilgrim for your vocation!"

At last, I thought, thankful to this canny Scot, this is a brilliant way out of my quandary. So I was nodding vigorously in accord with his analysis and all around that good crowd was clapping joyously.

"How lucky it is for us having you on board" said that monk who first bid 'good day'. "Now that our pilgrims know you as a holy human, you must join us straight away by coming to Swindon and our global mobilisation. Always room for additional communicants, you know. Stay on board and sing and pray and worship with us."

This was not what I had in mind at all. I had to find a way to abscond as soon as this train got to Slough. It had run past Southall a short duration ago, and I thought I ought to stand by a pair of sliding doors so that I could jump out rapidly on arrival at my stop. But to put my captors off worrying I would rush away, I was smiling and nodding and shaking hands all round. Finally as soon as our train ground to a halt in Slough, I did a lightning bolt out of that doorway and ran madly along that platform, with anxious or angry shouts coming from that band of pilgrims. I was away at last, wiping my brow, thanking my lucky stars, and fairly happy that I was in fact a Trappist monk.

It was now important to avoid an unpunctual arrival at Doctor Mark Smith's clinic in his local hospital, so I took a black cab from Slough station, having put down in writing its location on a pad to show to my taxi man. In this way I had no obligation to say any words to him. A rapid run through light traffic, a good tip on arrival and a big grin back was a fitting conclusion to an unusual and difficult transit from London.

From my childhood days, I can affirm that a visit to a doctor was always a worrying affair. I usually put it off as long as I could, claiming in a cowardly way that I was not truly sick, it was just a blip, a hiccup, a slight discomfort that would quickly pass away and so forth. But on this particular occasion, it was a critical situation I was in, and so I just had to go through with it. Thus with my wrist watch slowly coming up to two o'clock, I was at last in that doctor's consultation unit, quaking about what was about to occur.

I think that Doctor Smith's assistant, who saw my anxious look as I got out of a lift on his floor and said who I was, had an inkling of my fright. That kind lady, smiling warmly, said softly that I should not worry but sit calmly for a short duration in his waiting room. Doctor Smith was looking forward to solving my difficulty. I did pick up and thumb through an old sports journal from a rack but found I could not focus on it. I did not wait for long. Coming out of his consultation room to join us, Doctor Smith had a way with him that was cordial and harmonious, holding out his hand with a warm familiar grin.

"Paul Morrison? Good to know you. This way, if you don't mind".

Sitting comfortably in a Victorian mahogany chair in his stylish study and looking at his wall-to-wall rows of books with shiny traditional old black or brown pigskin bindings and bold gold titling, I was happy to submit to his scrutiny. Doctor Smith had to start his analysis of my curious condition by proposing that, initially anyway, I should avoid talking and copy down my input for his inquiry and scrutiny in writing. I was most happy with this approach. Probing into my past, asking if this was my first such attack, my doctor, glancing at my manuscript, took down in his tiny writing, copious facts, topics and thoughts. Following this "grilling" in a kindly way with various forms of word play, and an x-ray of my vocal chords, I was put into a dark room for a quantity of scans of my brain. Finally Doctor Smith sat down to impart a summary of his conclusions so far.

"I cannot find anything particularly worrying physically. And your brain shows no signs of injury or trauma according to your various x-rays" was his first point. "But yours is a fascinating and highly unusual condition. I found it fairly difficult in fact to form a sound diagnosis and I am opting for your having a psychological and not a physical condition. It's probably a form of dysphasia—an inability to say particular words, through vocal dysphonia or dysprosody—a loss of rhythm of words.

"I saw a curious thing during our bit of fun with you talking and partaking in various sorts of word-play just now. You said many words without difficulty until a block would occur, bringing you to a rapid halt. All this was forcing my mind to think back to days of my youth as a junior doctor in training in a hospital in Paris and occasionally saw this abnormality. It was known as lipogrammatical oblivion. But in this country it is practically unknown, though surprisingly its contagion is growing. I will just show you, if you do not mind, what this is, by playing out again a small bit of fun with you. A straightforward Q and A which you might find childish but it will show, I think, how this particular condition can virtually stop normal communication. Is that O.K?"

"O.K." I said, suspiciously.

"What word do you think of, if I say 'A slow animal on which Christ sat to go into that Holy City in anticipation of his crucifixion'?"

"Ass" I said.

"Right. Now how about 'a curvy tropical fruit with a sunny colour and a thick skin'?"

"Banana"

"Good. I'll carry on, if I may. 'What's that big country just north of USA'?"

"Canada" I said. But I was starting to think 'What *is* this childish rubbish all about?'

"You'll soon find out why I'm doing this" Doctor Smith was obviously picking up my thoughts.

"Now 'Man's most faithful animal with which to go hunting or just for walks'?"

"Dog" I put in, trying not to yawn.

"How about this? 'An animal found in a zoo, with a long trunk and thick skin'".

Finding all this absurdity irritating, I was about to shout that analogous word out loud. But in fact I just could not in any way say that scrap of vocabulary—nothing. My mouth was stuck, my lips solid. I was totally dumb. It was scary.

But my doctor was smiling now as if a hunch of his had paid off.

"I think you and I just had proof of my initial supposition—that your complaint is in fact that most common form of lipogrammatical dysphasia. Did you not grasp that you find your block occurs as you try pronouncing any word containing what I am having to call 'that fifth sign of our abc'? 'D' is a possibility for you to say and so is 'F' but not that poor guy amidships. A gigantic no-no! Just try saying what country you inhabit."

". . . ." Good Lord! Doctor Smith was spot on—a total block.

"And what country has Tokyo as capital?" "Japan!" I said naturally. I had to admit Doctor Smith's diagnosis was a distinct probability. But what could I do to attain normality again?

That good doctor saw what I was thinking, adding: "Sadly I cannot put forward any quick or automatic solution to your most unusual condition. It could vanish for good just as swiftly as it hit you. For now, you must constantly look for and try only using words *without* that fatal sign or just put down things in writing. You will always find trying to talk difficult in social situations, as you can say 'no' all right but obviously you cannot possibly say that crucially important opposing affirmation. I could try hypnosis on you but for now I am proposing two actions which I trust will assist you.

"First of all, you should contact an organisation that knows this syndromic condition backwards—Oulipo. It was born in Paris a good many moons ago but it has a branch in London which I think could assist you to find a way through in what in fact for you is a sort of word play. This cordial group has lots of inspiration and imagination, and would wallow in coming to your aid, I think, and in assisting you to find a lasting solution. In fact a famous Gallic virtuoso was part of that original Oulipo group (I cannot try giving you his ID as it is full of that fatal sign), a brilliant author of an amusing opus in his own lingo, totally without using that 'partial round form with a horizontal bar across'. And this particular book has had a most valid translation into our lingo which you could always consult to aid you in picking out OK words to say."

Doctor Smith was writing out contact information, as I cut in:

"And action 2. What do I do?" I was avoiding that catastrophic 'fifth sign' as I was looking for words. A difficult task, but it was working!

That doctor was smiling now. "Action 2, as you put it, is writing a book. You must try to turn into an author. Construct an opus in your own hand, without on any occasion using that fatal "fifth". Focussing on this task will assist you in your constant hunt for words, as you go communicating out into our world. And guard it all scrupulously as I'll want to go through that magnum opus with you at your following visit as part of your transformation back to normality. Call my P.A. in a month or so to fix a forthcoming consultation. And good luck!"

Aboard that slow British Rail train back to London, which, in contrast to my outward trip was an oasis of tranquillity, hardly a third full with normal local folk studiously avoiding any talking, I took stock of my situation and all that Doctor Smith was advising. That good man was smart to pinpoint what was causing my partial vocal block but had not found out strictly why. And what was my condition again? Lip . . . oh, not lipstick I think. Many a slip from cup to lip, as is commonly said. No, it's all to do with lipograms. I am a victim of lipograms. Still, with application, it should not turn out too difficult to avoid that untoward rascal in our abc if I follow his instructions. Authorship of a book totally without it should turn out an amusing and stimulating activity. But abruptly a frightful thought hit my mind. What about my PC? That most obligatory tool. That constant contact for chatting with my crowd of chums. Will it work? I do not think Microsoft has such a thing as D-mail or F-mail. Catastrophic!

III

Dipping my croissant into my cappuccino that following cool cloudy Monday morning, cat on lap, I got down to planning how I would approach composing that obligatory diary or journal or biography or plain story, without that humbug sign, according to Doctor Smith's diktat. I was no born wordsmith. Writing was not my skill, not now nor back in my youth. In days past, I would go as far as I could to try to avoid scribbling thank-you mail to aunts for Christmas gifts. As a young lad in a Boy Scout troop, I studiously did a log about various outings—cycling up to Stratford-upon-Avon or camping in Holland. Usual childish rubbish I am afraid to say.

But now, as an adult, that thought of turning into an author was intriguing. You may know how it is. You want to start that book, that magnum opus always dormant in your thoughts, your pass to glorious popularity and lots of cash, but your inspiration just won't spark. Your mind is dim, your brain is numb, your imagination totally void. Such a pity! You would think your skull was always full of surprising and thrilling plots, many an amazingly unfamiliar approach, an array of dramatic twists and turns to a story, unusual vocabulary, but no, as you launch into action, it all shrinks into nothing, try as you might to sustain it.

I did try my hand at writing on a particular occasion in my youth with a non-fiction work—a history of birth control in this country. All a bit taboo for an upright church-going lad. I was going to call it 'Copulation Without Population' (about condoms and also pills as hazards to mankind) but I did not finish it for lack of motivation and unsatisfactory collaboration, in fact zilch input from all and sundry—and our pastor was aghast.

To cut a long story short, if I may borrow that saying, and I am carrying on a bit, I did not know how to start my lipogrammatical book with a valid introductory gambit of my own, to say nothing about working painstakingly through to finishing a world class yarn. I finally had a smart thought. Why not simply try to obtain stimulation from world class authors who might furnish an intriguing approach for my opus or anyway show a good way through my fix? I should look hard for stimulus in such classic or popular books as I own among that copious bibliographic array in my study.

Should I turn to Conrad or Galsworthy or Kipling? Consult Iris Murdoch, Virginia Woolf or Roald Dahl? Or could I find my saviour in that author known in full as Vidiadhar Surajprasad Naipaul—no sign of no-no signs with him, don't you think? Finally I thought my most promising start was in fact with that immortal bard from Stratford-upon-Avon. Could our grand chum William, with all his dramas, supply that magic spark? And would I find a good way of adapting that prolixity of good copy of his to my grim world which was totally lacking in that all important fifth sign?

I hit upon a brilliant way forward by taking down my voluminous dictionary of famous quotations in which I sought an accumulation of truly inspiring copy for practising a valid adaptation.

Soon I was in full flight, analysing orations in works by our prolific national playwright, adjusting many a familiar group of words said by that Danish king's son, and also adapting various of William's most famous lyrics:

'Living or dying, that is what I am asking all about'

A bit obvious but not bad! I'll try again:

'Pop off to a woman's holy institution! Why would you fancy giving birth to sinful humans?'

'A nag . . . no . . . a cavalry animal . . . no . . . a stallion . . . that's good. *'A stallion, a stallion, my dominion for a stallion!'* That's going too far. I could just stay with *'kingdom*'! I had no obligation to supplant all words in a quotation. Only vocal villains.

Passing now on to a play which I could only call *'As You Fancy It'*, I was scribbling away, with inspiration coming through quick and fast:

'All this world's a dramatic platform, and all its boys and girls only actors'

This was going amazingly. And I was having fun.

'Now is that frigidity of our unhappy disposition changing into glorious sunny warmth, thanks to this son of York'

'Chums, Romans, rural folk, turn your aural organs my way. I am with you to drop Julius down a pit, not to slap him on his back'.

Stylistically a triumph, I was thinking, proud of my writing skills, and most importantly, proof that I was savvy in limiting my copy to using a, i, o, u and y. Also Y? Why not! But to carry on practising, I thought I should say *ciao* to that Bard and pass on for stimulation to a distinct sort of author, political now, and not a classical wordsmith of drama. I did look at Karl Marx but could not warm to any of his communist outbursts. Winston Churchill was obviously an attraction too, so I had a go at his historical oration:—

> *'You and I shall fight on our coasts, on our landing grounds. Us lot shall fight on our grasslands and on our roads and fight in our hills, without giving in on any occasion'.*

I was truly happy now with my ability, in manipulating quotations from that group of classics, to avoid that humbug, that charlatan, that impostor, that traitor hiding within our abc, whilst still communicating plainly to all and sundry what I had to say. In fact I was sword in hand to start. But what sort of publication should I try producing? I had thought long and hard but could not think of a valid or intriguing plot for a play or a story and so finally had to opt for a biography—in fact an autobiography. I would start writing my own fascinating diary, in which I would, I trust, find it stimulating to log inch by inch my bumpy road back to normality. A first hand journal to furnish doctors throughout our world with original and apt insights into actually curing my most unusual malady.

Lastly but not unimportantly, I still had to fix upon a starting gambit to my story, an initial group of words so intriguing and original as to grab hold of any bookworm, who might start to dip into it, and to prompt him to carry on until its final closing word. I found that "missing link" in a book I had just put down. Sadly, my vocal block is making it an impossibility to say out loud what his public calls this socialist author or how his passport might list him—but his work was highly political. That radical giant had G.O. for initials and that first group of words from his famous fantasy about a nightmarish futuristic world was captivating:

"It was a bright cold day in April . . . . (In fact it is April as I am writing this!) And I would carry on . . . *and my clock was striking . . . "*

Brilliant! I'll work with that tantalising introduction as an intriguing way into this, my own most unusual autobiography. How I got into this fix and how I'll try to find a way out of it. If at all!

IV

Though it is now long past midnight, I must just sit down and start writing part four of my lipogrammatical diary. I am in fact so angry that I cannot wait until tomorrow to do so. I could in no way simply fall on my divan right now and calmly drop off, with my mind in such turmoil. So much for my plan to pass a compulsory half hour of a morning updating my biography, following Doctor Smith's instructions! I must launch into it right now at this witching hour.

To put it frankly today was an awful day. In fact, not to put too sharp a point on it, today was a bloody awful day. Frustrating, humiliating, catastrophic! But wait an instant, fair's fair, not totally disastrous. I must start coming down to ground with a bump as I do admit that things did all start calmly.

In fact I got up with that famous lark, bright and happy and I was fit for action. It was a mild sunny morning—surprisingly for April. Following all that trauma and activity of past days, I found it most comforting just to climb into my old hammock, hanging from that Victorian oak down in my small grassy back yard, to think hard and plan how to claw my way up that tricky inclination to normality. Rocking slowly, I put down in writing my to-do list: Major points. First: contact Lisa and do all I could to win that lady back. Part two: work out how to do my job this coming night in Luigi's, by finding out how to chat to patrons, noting down ways of talking about this or that dish, passing on such options to our flamboyant cook and finally coping with bills—and tips!

Starting with sorting things out with Lisa? First priority: I just had to call my florist and buy and ship a glorious bunch of blooms with a stylish romantic card containing my fond thoughts and also broadly outlining my affliction and all that Doctor Smith had said about solving my condition. I would also call Lisa at work around midday with an invitation to a cosy gastronomic visit to a top multi-star culinary attraction on Friday night. But most important for winning Lisa back, I had to work hard on amplifying my vocabulary so that I could start talking in a distinct and normal sounding way. My plan for doing this was writing down and committing to mind a long list of groups of words, chit-chat, small talk, gossip, opinions, wit and jocularity, charm, humour, admiration, proposals (not that sort, just for now!), in fact a total gamut of oral communication without you know what.

I had a slow start but fairly soon, going backwards and forwards through my dictionary and tapping into my skill in doing crosswords, I was off and running, building groups of OK words and scribbling down in black ink such bits of communication which I would imprint on my mind.

"Ah Lisa, you look so smart today. That outfit suits you fantastically"

"I am sorry I was not at all on form for your visit last Saturday. Silly, as I was missing you. And I did find your photos truly amazing. You must try to publish a book."

"Doctor Smith is a fantastic guy and his diagnosis was spot-on. My brain just will not allow my using any word with that sign in our "abc" which sits twixt "d" and "f".

Silly, isn't it? But I will surmount it all by following all his instructions. You must not think I am totally dumb."

I got prodigious satisfaction from composing and writing down all such bits of colloquy, and I soon had a vast list of sundry topics. Lisa was bound to go along with it all, I thought. It was my plan to call my darling around midday and put it all on trial.

Rubbing my hands with gusto, I swung calmly to and fro for almost half an hour, basking in that comforting sunlight. And I was starting to think about my job at Luigi's and draw up a similar list of word groups for using at work tonight. It soon struck my mind that this would turn out a tough nut to crack.

If *pasta* and *salsa*, *pizza* and *ragu*, *macaroni*, *pollo* and *pomodori, ricotta, prosciutto* and *salami* would not tax my ability to talk, many a dish on our *carta* would. In Italian or in our British way of talking (as I must call it!) Should a patron ask what dish or two our cook was advising today and I was caught out, should I simply try looking dumb, and start communicating using signs? I could not simply say its adjoining group of digits. Trout with mushrooms was fifty two and Pork in milk was sixty four. But this would not work as a vast majority of digits was out of bounds for my vocalisation. In fact I would just point out words on my list.

A quick look at my watch and I saw it was approaching midday—a good timing to call Lisa who normally had a sandwich for a quick lunch at this hour, prior to going out for a short walk to a 'cash and carry' to do a bit of shopping. Back in my sitting room and just slightly shaky, with my word lists and talk plans in hand, I got hold of my Nokia and gritting my molars tightly, rang.

"Natural World Tourism. Good day"

"Could I talk to Lisa Johnston? If you don't mind. Thank you"

"Sorry I can't pass you Lisa, as all our staff is caught up in a brainstorming all day. Can you call back as from 4 pm?"

"Right. Many thanks".

I was civil to that switchboard lady but was a touch cross about having to wait to chat with Lisa again. How should I pass what would probably turn out a long frustrating four hour stint? Think up additional Q and A's in my quaint idiom? Possibly. But first I had to down a stiff drink—a shot of Scotch to build up spirits, don't you think? Why not! Taking a cut crystal glass from my drinks cupboard I put in a good inch of liquid Highland ambrosia and was quickly calm and warm within. Mmm, what an aroma, this truly is a godly spirit! Mmmmm! . . . . Again? Just a tiny dram, no? Don't mind if I do . . .

It was not until half past four that I was coming to from a most profound nap. It was not just forty winks! I was not proud of my foolish action in partaking of a drink too far and had a blind panic that I would possibly find out that I was too tardy now to catch Lisa still at work.

Rushing to pick up my communication apparatus and punching in digits as if I was crazy, I got through. I was in luck as that NWT switchboard was still working and I was told that Lisa was still taking calls. With my voluminous crib containing all my lists of OK word groups, sayings and licit oral communication in my right hand, I was in orbit:

"Hi Lisa, this is Paul. How you doing? I do miss you, you know."

Lisa was frigid and wary. "Oh! So you can talk again now."

"Lisa, I'm so sorry for what I said, or for what I didn't say, but I was . . . ill . . . (long gap) . . . Your stock of photos was just brilliant, you know."

It was not going smoothly, as Lisa abruptly cut in:

"You still sound funny, not totally with it at all. So what do you want? I'm right up to my chin with a proposal for a two-month Pacific study into Japan's whaling plans and I cannot go wasting hours talking to a clown."

Doom and gloom but, trying to show normality, I said:

"I saw a world-famous doctor with a diploma on my condition on Sunday last in Slough who did a thorough analysis. His diagnosis was that I had what is known as a lipogrammatical hiatus in communication. My vocal bits work satisfactorily, my hang up is in my brain. I can talk but I just cannot say a particular group of words."

"Paul, what *is* this rubbish?"

"Lisa, I know it's all a frightful complication but I am saying nothing but plain truth. I'm not playing around. This *is* an unusual affliction but it is known to doctors. I am truly ill but my condition can vanish as quickly as I caught it. May I just link up with you to lay it all out?"

Not a sound from Lisa apart from a cynical snort. Obviously, I had to vary my approach.

"Look, how about us both going out for a cosy talk about it all this coming Saturday, with a spot of that fantastic cooking at our usual haunt—now it's got two stars—*La Maison du Vin*. I won't act foolishly, on my honour! No talk of work or my nutty condition."

A sigh and a small laugh from Lisa and my optimism was starting to grow.

"That sounds fun, but I'm afraid it's my Grandma's birthday that day with a big party down in Brighton for all my family. Pity!"

"I know!" I cut in, my spirits buoyant now. "So what if us two go for a quick romantic trip to Paris, say, in a fortnight? You and I could book first class on that fast train from St Pancras, with all that bubbly on board, and stay as last spring at that cosy Right Bank mansion. *Aux Jardins du Marais*, wasn't it?, with its stunning courtyard and its saucy art on show on all its floors, just fifty yards from Picasso's famous flat."

I thought I had won now, as Lisa gushingly put in:

"O.K. Paul, but on a strict condition. That you drop all that rubbish and talk normally. I can't stand silly word-play. It's too irritating! Is that plain? Will you do it?"

In panic, it struck my foolishly optimistic brain that, paraphrasing or not—as my good doctor had said—I just could not bring out that short common word of affirmation.

"Aha!" was all I could do.

"No, Paul, don't start that rubbish again. Will you simply say that tiny word?"

"I will!"

Lisa was now showing distinct signs of irritation. "Can't you talk normally? I'm asking you just to say that obvious word that starts with 'y'. Or is it that you want to say 'no'?

I was panicking now. "No, it's not 'no'."

"Right, so if it's not 'no', what is it?"

"Lisa. It's just 'not no' as I don't want to say 'no' but I simply cannot say that opposing word to 'no'. So I'm *not* saying 'no' and I *am* saying 'not no'. Is that obvious, now—or no?

Building up to a paroxysm of fury, my loving lady was now paranoid.

"Paul, that is IT! A final straw! I cannot stand your irritating, childish, absurd, farcical, ridiculous, idiotic load of rubbish. I am finishing with you this instant. I'm giving it to you straight up and down. Do I want to go with a fool such as you to Paris? No, a thousand fold! Do I want to go out dining with an idiot such as you? No, a million fold. That's it, Paul. Curtains!" A loud click brought all that initially promising conciliation to an abrupt and tragic conclusion.

Fast forward now two and a bit hours and surprisingly, but happily, my mood is calm and lucid again. Far from still harbouring any black thoughts about Lisa's angry outburst, I am totally wound up now for doing a grand job as Luigi's minion and surviving that forthcoming night's task in hand. I am in fact found this instant walking to work briskly from my flat to our local station with a strong conviction that with all my wordlists (which I am still holding tight, softly chanting or adding to) and all my intuition, I can win through. A cool light invigorating wind uplifts my spirits.

A half hour on and I am not in such a good mood. For I am on board a hot, odorous and ludicrously busy Piccadilly train, trying to commit to mind all my sayings and gambits. A distinctly difficult activity as I am in an almighty squash, stuck flat against a pair of sliding doors by a loud jovial crowd of young black musicians playing gongs, banjos and harmonicas and passing a hat around for contributions to a charity for poor African orphans in Tanzania or Zambia or Somalia or Madagascar or Angola or was it Ghana? I didn't find out.

Arriving at Kings Cross station, I just had to alight and go up and outdoors and grab a lungful of cool invigorating night air by abandoning that madding crowd and carrying on by foot to Luigi's in Farringdon. I thought I would just waltz along, chanting out loud all my bits of culinary vocabulary (with no sign of that sign, obviously!).

But alas, I found to my horror that it was now raining cats and dogs, a total downpour, and as I had foolishly not brought a raincoat, nor a brolly, I quickly got a right royal soaking. I ran as fast as I could, splashing through that rising flood. My hair was stuck down across my brow, with raindrops trickling down my collar and through to my back, my clothing dripping and drooping, as I, awash now from top to tail, was finally making my way into Luigi's. I was hoping to God that Luigi was not, as usual, standing on guard in his doorway, nodding languidly at his staff and smiling warmly at his patrons. But as I ran up, I saw Luigi was on duty up front and so would strongly frown upon my condition—risking a disastrous start to what could build up to a catastrophic night. *Il capo* was, and it did.

Without saying a word but with a brutal look of disapproval, Luigi thrust a bunch of cotton napkins into my hands, so that I could dry my hair and swab my suit, and also parts of that day's *La Stampa* for wiping out my smart black boots. It did cross my mind that I might just try to say a word or two to him about my vocal condition, but I hastily had to stop short at his ominous look. Could I pull it all off and do a night's normal work?

My stomach was starting to twitch with worry but without warning I thought that I had found a brilliant solution. I would simply say to all and sundry (through signs if I had to) that on account of all that rain, I had in fact lost my vocal faculty and could just about mouth an odd word or two, softly and sparingly, but occasionally would stop making sounds and start making hand signals. If any local word was taboo, I could also opt for an occasional Italian match *pianissimo,* as a way out. Luigi was always in favour of all of his staff using his own idiom—and our patrons too. This was promising!

Looking dry and tidy by now, I was last, as usual, to join all staff at Luigi's "tonight's culinary status" summary, or as us lot would simply call it—"what's on and what's off". Luigi was buoyant tonight, informing us all that it was a full booking in our *trattoria*, our main dish array was duck or rabbit or lamb—to say nothing of our usual various sorts of pasta and ravioli (I was noting down with joy my ability in coping with all such OK words!) But now with patrons starting to turn up, my trial was looming.

And do you know, starting off was not difficult at all! My first contact was with two charming old folk, habitual patrons, a dwarfish old man with long gold locks and his lady with curly black hair, both big fans of Italy and its food, happy *parlando italiano,* smiling at my soft vocal outburst of *Ciao, signori,* and choosing (also in Italian) *una birra* and *un Cinzano bianco.* To my inquiry "What can I bring you from *la carta?"* I was again lucky. Both had *Prosciutto con Fichi* to start, and to follow, it was *Pollo con Rosmarino* for *la signora* and for him *Stufatino alla Romana.* Amazing! No sign of any vocal snag in all that. Things going brilliantly—so far!

As for choosing drinks from our list, I was making signals that I could not talk loudly, tapping my hand against my mouth and saying "laryngitis", nodding and pointing to two options in my black plastic list—36 and 42. Both took on board my proposal, smiling happily, and so I had won that first trial of my ability to do my job.

Fast forward an hour, with our *trattoria* now virtually full, and I was coping skilfully with this mix of schoolboy Italian, artificial loss of vocal communication and using hand signals, managing both patrons and cooks. Until, that is, to my horror I caught sight of an all too familiar group of loud City louts, arriving straight from its out-of-hours trading floor, with Luigi disastrously motioning that mob to sit in a solitary gap in my part of our dining room.

A foul bunch, high on substantial financial gains throughout that day's trading—and no doubt on additional stimulation—cannabis? opium? or a similar comforting drug—who knows? Its boss man was as always highly vocal:

"That's our big black Jaguar out in front, just park it for us, would you, my good man?" This was said to old Paolo by our front door. And to our boss . . .

"Hi, Luigi, you old bastard, just bring two jars of your top bubbly, would you? Us lot want to toast big, big winnings today".

Pushing blindly through and arriving in my domain, this uncouth group sat down in a good spot, by a window with a vista of our patio—as a loud shouting match was starting up. And with Luigi hastily following with two magnums of that sparkling ambrosia.

"Wow! What a day, huh, you guys? Up and up in bounds of sixty points all bloody day—it wouldn't stop. I sold all my BT straight away this morning and got 40 grand and I still had my coat on—hadn't sat down. And on and on. Apart from that CAC, which took a whack. Down 56. Bloody frogs!"

"Too right, old son! But at two pm, with that data on US factory activity, did you watch that sodding Dow? Wow!"

"Bow wow, you dog—barking mad, that's you! You didn't buy what I said. Goldman Sachs and WPP. No complaints on my part. I also had a killing with Gold and Oils. And you, Sid. What about your Industrials and Transport? Was that a good trip?"

"No, I wouldn't touch that particular lot. Too cautious, too rigid—and from now on I plan to avoid any banking stock too. City analysts just won't back that stuff nowadays. A crunch is on its way again. So says J P Morgan. But I did play with Bonds. And also got into Dollars, Pounds and also South African Rand. That was grand!"

"Yup! Too right, son! To win, my good chum, you must always act hungry."

"Hungry! Who said hungry? I'm f—ing starving." It was "boss man" again, downing his third glass of Mumm Grand Brut, taking control and looking for staff to satisfy his crowd of gluttons. And quickly. That poor individual was, catastrophically, yours truly. With disdain and gloom, I slid up to start taking down this group's copious blow-out. Making signs and with odd words, I told that group about my lost vocal chords and inability to talk loudly and I did try my Italian "solution" to this particular condition but got no sympathy from such a ploy.

"Whatsat? Talk loudly, you idiot. And in British, if you don't mind. Drop this Italian mumbo jumbo'. "Big Mouth" standing up and shouting, ran down a list of what food and drinks to bring, adding tauntingly, as if I was stupid: "Hungry, hungry, *rapidissimo*, O.K?"

By now I was livid, but could not show it and just had to humour that bunch. I saw that my charming old pair of patrons was moving off, quickly vacating our grill room with a sad look and similar patrons, bills paid, sliding away to avoid that growing turmoil. But our trattoria was still fairly full and I had much work to do, with many a dish to bring out. I had a lot of sympathy now for all Luigi's good patrons calmly sitting around waiting and having to put up with that bunch of yobbos cursing and complaining loudly about how slow it all was. Why did not Luigi simply throw that lot out?

Four Dutch tourists, just a yard or two from that diabolical bunch, calmly sat in anticipation of giant portions of *pasta con pomidori* which I was at last carrying out from our frantically busy cook. Sliding and twisting my way through all that throng sitting in such tightly knit groups, with my hands up high, balancing a tray with such big bowls of food, I was slowly approaching my goal. What was to follow was nothing short of catastrophic—in fact, my nadir.

I could not avoid brushing past that loud City crowd with my load. "Aha, that's probably ours—at long last! Look, stop, that's all for us". Arriving in front of that lot, I said that it wasn't. Quickly a foot was stuck out so that I would stop in my tracks, but I was not conscious of it. I saw it all in slow motion as I was tripping forward—my four portions of Luigi's luscious Italian pasta and its rich colourful oily garnish flying up and coming down all across that City group's classy mohair suits.

A bloodcurdling angry howl rang out from that bunch, in addition to a long list of filthy words. (Such as "H*ly Sh*t! Which though I could, I will not print out in full!) Rabid hands took a firm hold of my collar, fists hit my chin and body and a chair was brought down on my skull. Furious in turn, I was not going to submit to such an attack without a fight and hitting back, I laid a mighty punch on Big Mouth's stubbly chin. Blood burst out from his vulgar mouth. Bingo!

In an instant Luigi was at hand to stop our fight, pulling us apart and shouting to all to calm down.

"This suit cost a grand, you bastard" was Big Mouth's indignant cry, picking or flicking off bits of food from its light brown fabric and wiping his dirty lips with his hand.

Luigi too had a flaming look, turning my way and loudly announcing it was obviously all my fault. I was guilty of gross, shabby, scandalous actions towards his good patrons, unworthy of his *casa* and in saying so, in front of all and sundry, it was a prodigious public sacking. I had no opportunity to put forth my own account of that affray.

"Go wait in our back room, you big fool. I will do your job from now on until closing. With our doors finally shut, I will pay you and hand you your cards. Sit down now, all you good patrons"

You must know what mood I was in as I sat waiting in hiding, whilst all was calm again without. Luigi had in fact told that city crowd that as an apology, all costs would go back to him, with him also not charging for lunch for a fortnight.

I had to sit fuming in that back room until past midnight. Finally with all now still and locking his takings away, Luigi slid through that door for our final discussion, saying how sad it was to part in such a way, as my approach to working was to his mind upright, trustworthy, brisk, smart . . . (Why was my boss so blooming laudatory, if sacking was still on his mind?) . . . good and loyal and rapid.

But . . . in his book, anybody providing custom is always right, including occasions on which it is that rascal who is at fault. So that was it—sad but compulsory. Luigi put into my hands two month's salary and a tin full of tips and said *ciao* with a warm Italian hug. It was hard not to hug him back as I took off. I was fond of that old bastard.

Back in that London night air, with my mind in turmoil, I had to find a way of going back to my flat with probably no public transport still running. Damnation, I thought, shaking my tin of cash, I'll just go back by black cab. A long run—but I'm worth it! Luckily at that instant, coming down that road, I saw a bright "vacant" roof light on an approaching taxi and I stuck my hand up to stop it.

"Going far, guv'nor?"

"Wandsworth"

"Good, jump in! Foul night, innit?"

V

Good morning, all! Following last night's calamity, I am in a surprisingly good mood today, taking things calmly and not showing any panic or worry.

Having got up a good two hours following what is my norm (with no job to do, no alarm clock!), I am sitting by my window, looking out on my sunny suburban road with not a cloud in sight, such a transformation following last night's downpour. OK, I admit it, things should look grim. No job, plus no girl, plus no ability to talk normally, that's not a cosy situation to occupy. But I just know that if I can hang on in with optimism and luck, I will hit on a brilliant way out of all my sorrows.

In addition my digital radio is on a classical music station which is playing softly a string of soothing Italian standards—Vivaldi, Scarlatti, also compositions by Gastrucci, if I'm not wrong. It all flows calmly across my mind to banish any morbid disposition. And I must admit that that gift of six thousand pounds I got last month from my Aunt Marion's will and which is still in its totality in my savings account with Lloyds TSB bank should shun that wolf from my door for a good four months or so.

And finally I am sitting at my PC typing wildly, surfing with gusto and looking for a brilliant way forward from among a host of job options that I am finding. Who wants a dumb, poorly paid occupation in a boring London trattoria anyway, if you can find an atypical stimulating job, brilliantly paid, possibly abroad? I am finding many such posts going and am writing down a list of options to follow up on—thirty in fact in my first hour.

A dull clunk in my hallway and it's a signal that my postman has just stuck copious mail through my box. I wait first to finish my surfing and job hunting and go to pick it up. As usual I quickly discard all that annoying junk—promotional handouts, round robins and charity solicitations—but among it all I find post from Doctor Mark Smith. Apart from his instructions on what drugs to try and contact data for a local GP whom I could consult in a hurry, it also contains full background on Oulipo's UK organisation, its board, its policy, and in particular its up-and-coming activity list. What follows was good tidings:

> *"If you wish to sit in on an Oulipo group that is focussing on your lipogrammatical complaint in particular, go along to an AGM and 'cultural symposium' it will hold tomorrow (Saturday) at noon (isn't that handy?) in a dark and dusty waiting room on platform 2 of Clapham Junction railway station. You must know it. It's in South London. This group is good fun and always happy to absorb visitors with your sort of condition who might think of joining. (Annual subscription is only £6—a bargain!) Got a railcard? If so, you won't pay for a platform pass. Good luck."*

First class timing! And a most unusual location—but this is a most unusual organisation.

Going back to my PC, I thank my doctor profoundly and opt for calling it a day. I log out and am told by Microsoft:

"Windows is shutting down" . . . . And so am I. Adios, I'll talk to you tomorrow.

*　　*　　*

My train on that short run to Clapham Junction had standing room only, and so on arriving, I thought I would just stop and chill out for an instant or two on that windy platform and swallow many lungfuls of cool brisk air and not go looking straightaway for that Oulipo crowd. So I just sat down on a vacant old handcart lying around, and slowly took in that broad panorama of what was, without any doubt, a giant railway station. Long curving platforms, vast twisting iron tracks tracing out north and south, joining up and parting far away up towards a misty horizon, trains continuously stopping, starting or just zooming past, signals flashing, busy sounds of clunking and humming and rattling and roaring. And all this brought back abruptly and vividly to my mind a sad but warm nostalgia.

It must sound silly to say it, but in fact I found I was thinking, from my days at my grammar school, (pity it was not a lipogrammar school!) about that boring Gallic author, Proust and his autobiographical book in which it was that famous small ovoid sugary pastry of his, (containing flour, almonds, vanilla and with a citrus fruit flavour) which was such a jog to his mind in conjuring up poignant days of lost youth. I was having a similar subconscious flashback. For my part, this particular railway panorama was calling forth from my unconscious a vivid portrayal of my good old Grandpa John, who throughout his days had a driving passion for railways and trains and who could not stop talking ad infinitum to all and sundry about that "iron road" and all that was passing along it. A profusion of yarns, topics, bits of gossip, rumours or thrills.

I am picturing him now narrating parrot-fashion, as was his wont, all about a warm invitation from old Patrick Murphy, a signalman in his box in Southall, for my granddad as a small lad to join him in his "grandstand" and watch Bristol bound trains with a fabulous GWR loco up front, pounding down from Paddington and racing past.

"Look Pat, a king, a king", young Grandpa would shout. And so it was—King Class 6002, King William IV—a truly royal shining colossus, pistons thumping and hissing and its stack pumping out a long billowing smoky signal thrusting up, up into that charcoal sky.

Or I was told about how as a young pilgrim, calling in on railway workshops in Didcot, making that trip in Third Class (or occasionally, not having cash to pay his way, hiding in a guard's van) with his Ian Allan books with lists of train digits in his backpack, Grandpa would pass all day drooling in admiration at such an amazing accumulation of iron stallions. Or how that good soul in his sad final days would wring his hands and mourn *past* days of railway glory, now lost for good. An outcry against that brutal post-war annihilation of all such traditional locos, icons of past days of British manufacturing inspiration, quality and glory—mostly ignominiously sold off for scrap by foolish politicians favouring motorways to that iron road, motor cars to Pullman cars, gas stations to railway stations. Downcast, Grandpa would croak in his final days, that Isambard Kingdom was now without doubt turning in his tomb . . . .

"Sorry sir, but I want to start using this cart".

That sad solicitation brought my mind sharply back to why I was at Clapham Junction at all and to my task in hand. My vivid flashback to past railway glory was quickly fading away and I found that I too was looking sadly around at today's railway—its dismal platforms, its functional bog standard train units gliding along from a to b, a jump in/jump out sort of transportation, utilitarian but so boring. I cannot say that today's kids show any passion for this world now. And that rail trip I did to Slough was just ghastly. Across my mind ran that famous quotation I obviously had to adapt:

"Our past is an outlandish country; mankind is doing things in its own distinct way in that location". (Not a bad try, was it?)

Apologising, I got up smartly to go. Glancing at my watch, I saw that my Oulipo rally was about to start and so I ran smartly off towards a stairway to cross tracks and find its location. I was at last about to find out if this singular occult organisation could in any way put my mind back on a rapid track to normality.

VI

"Hold tight. This is it!" Such is what I was thinking, as I was tramping upstairs, crossing four lots of tracks and coming down a dusty stairway to finally put foot on Platform 2. It was that instant of truth. My first contact with Oulipo, at last. But will this crowd of wordsmiths whom I am now about to join, know ways of solving my linguistic block? Will I find all its participants with an ability to talk in a smooth and loquacious way—continuously and normally?

In particular, will I actually find out from this crowd about any sort of psychiatry, drug, prophylactic, stimulant, narcotic or hypnotism—anything—as a spur to going back to straightforward forms of communication? Put succinctly, how far can this group possibly assist in my accomplishing a trio of goals: to talk normally again, to land a good satisfying highly paid job and to win back Lisa's favours.

Although I was looking all around this platform, I could not find any signboard indicating a waiting room, but what I did catch sight of was a frightful shock. It was a big digital station clock hanging down just in front, clicking away and indicating that it was in fact almost half past midday and that I was way out in my timing for this all important first contact with Oulipo at noon. My cousin's old Victorian gold watch which I always found was fun to sport on important occasions such as this outing, had ground to a halt half an hour ago, for want of winding up fully, with its two hands pointing straight upwards. Just my luck!

Quick, quick! How could I find this all-important room? Nobody was around in this totally vacant part of this station to ask—no staff, in fact not a solitary human was in sight. So I had to rush frantically around, gazing window by window into totally dark rooms containing not a soul, nothing. Until as I was almost giving up, practically out of sight, right up front on that platform, I hit upon an anonymous looking door and through its dirty glass, I saw a crowd of folks. Found, at last!

Having shown a total lack of punctuality, I was too shy simply to crash in. In what way should I go about making my introduction and apologising for only turning up just now? I did not know. So I stood awkwardly at that door, gazing through that grubby window at what was going on within. But I was conscious that I would probably soon attract a watchful look from an individual participating in all that busy activity.

A crowd of fifty or sixty, mostly clad informally, sat on rows of chairs facing a tall man with a shock of curly auburn hair, standing in front of a giant flip chart and scribbling rapidly on it with a broad black tip. I could not catch a word of what that individual was actually saying, but I saw what was on his board:

Motto for all Fifth Columnists:
Sharing a common vision of working in unison and harmony

Fifth Columnists? What's this all about? What has this particular condition, of which I too am victim, got to do with communism? I thought that Oulipo was a non-political organisation, or so I was told. But it was not too hard to grasp what this alias was all about. Fifth Columnists, *that* must simply stand for an occult and fairly taciturn bunch of folks such as us, who talk funnily by missing out that fifth sign. Brilliant.

I also caught sight of a group of four fairly old patriarchal chaps, sitting around a circular dais on which stood a colourful floral display, an audio unit for playing CDs and also a giant dictionary (to look up synonyms, I was imagining). Possibly, Oulipo's chairman and his top officials.

In a flash, that door through which I was watching was flung outwards and an anxious looking man, staring mistrustfully, said: "What do you want?" Choosing all my words painstakingly (as this was my first trial at talking in public following my saga at Luigi's), I said: "Good day. I am Paul Morrison and I'm having difficulty with talking . . . hum . . . I saw Doctor Mark Smith um . . . and his diagnosis was that I had dysphonia and that Oulipo might assist in my um . . . and I ought to turn up with you today . . . umm . . . sorry I was not with you . . . umm . . . as it was starting"

I could not go on. But I was not having to, as all in that group, in particular its big guns, stood up smiling, hands thrust out warmly to grasp my own, saying how good it was that I was joining that organisation. I was struck dumb by such cordiality.

"Your condition is not unusual, you know. Thousands fall into this linguistic block of ours. Picking up and adapting to our Fifth Columnist sort of communication is not difficult. With our group, you can attain many ways of improving and building up your ability to talk."

"Nor is curing this indisposition an impossibility. Trust us. My aunt in Torquay had a sharp lipogram attack last autumn but has now got totally back to normal"

"Having this malady can turn out good fun too. It's surprising to say so. Lots of laughs, you know."

"Aha! An addition to our happy crowd"

"Un grand bonjour to our club!"

"Oh don't worry about that chap. Dominic hails from across that narrow strip of H2O, dividing us from Calais—and that Gallic nation!"

Bursts of laughing rang out following this last highly colourful proclamation, obviously coming from a postulant just starting to pick up how to talk in this Oulipo idiom.

I was shown to a vacant front row chair and told that Oulipo's chairman of lipogrammatical affairs was about to hold forth with his formal annual allocution. As this grand old man stood up to talk, that roomful was applauding vigorously. I was told that this was Doctor Piotr Abramovitch from a family of Russian origin, born in Moscow, but with Polish nationality who had taught Historical Linguistics at Oxford, knowing many unusual idioms, such as Sanskrit, Albanian, Bulgarian and Old Church Slavonic.

But this amazing scholar had abruptly caught our curious malady and on taking a sabbatical from his singular world of study, had sought to bypass all his blocks and obtrusions to normal communication by studying our condition profoundly and by joining and assisting in running its "first aid" syllabus in conjunction with his old varsity faculty.

His oratory was a triumph. Fluid, but with conviction, rich in vocabulary and good humour, Doctor Piotr ran through Oulipo's goals and annual work plan in a plain sailing fashion. I found I was following a smooth flow of words from a man with my complaint who was not glancing at any script and had no lists in writing at hand as a prompt (as I had to do in my job at Luigi's). I sat in rapt admiration. Could I possibly attain a similar skill in fluid and abundant communication? I'll just furnish you with a quick summary of his stirring words:

"Your board has sought to adopt an uncompromising approach towards making this affliction that haunts us today vanish from this world tomorrow. Although finding a way of totally curing this condition of ours is not fully obvious at this point, I know how much all of you firmly sign up to our policy of waging a constant war against it.

"To fight this constraint on a global basis and win is thus our singular goal and that is why our plan of maintaining contacts and joint trials in many parts of this world is so important. Our principal laboratory—with input from a working party of famous doctors studying aphasia and applying our six-part plan in various locations—has had a significant amount of luck among Fifth Columnists as it is customary, if amusing, now to call us folks.

"In our diagnostic stations in Washington, Sao Paulo, Jakarta, Madrid, Bombay and Accra, our staff has sought to bring to maturity a raft of actions all aiming at quickly diagnosing our complaint, pinpointing who is most at risk, halting its diffusion and finally aiding and instructing individuals with symptoms to know how to fight through and win. I call it simply "can do" vocabulary. I cannot wait.

"And finally, an additional highly involving proposal of ours was to start a study, as from this month, in collaboration with nations such as Japan, China and Saudi Arabia who as you all know do not follow us in using an ABC in writing and thus do not worry about our infamous fifth sign. Its ongoing aim is to pinpoint in such lands with singular forms of script, any linguistic paralysis similar to our own which has a link to any symbol or vocal sound in any idiom in which that particular population is communicating. Playback on all this fascinating inquiry is in two months—isn't that thrilling?

"I shall hand out a summary of all such various topics as soon as I finish, but I did want to say a last thing, which I hold as truly important for all you Fifth Columnists to think about, should you, on any occasion, sink into low spirits on account of your condition. Always, I say it again, *always* start taking comfort in your opportunity for actually *using* your complaint for artistic innovation. It is amazing how much any constraints in your mind can magnify—a thousand-fold—your artistic output. This is an undying mantra for anybody among us in Oulipo.

"Compositions in writing without that sign, which you allow to hatch and blossom in your mind using rhyming words, rhythm, scansion and a tight syllabic count can assist you in producing harmonious and imposing art, which will gain for you admiration from all and sundry and build you up morally. Go on, just try! Think Milton, think Wordsworth, Byron, Browning. I could go on and on, but I won't. I will just thank you and wish you lots of inspiration, lots of satisfaction, lots of good communication and lots of fun".

Tumultuous clapping burst forth throughout that room, with many of us standing, waving and hooting with joy. I was totally on board by this point. Following a handful of additional points of administration, our focus was now informal, with many a jovial activity and a string of amusing orations, locutions, antics, short talks or bright turns by various Oulipostulants, displaying with ability and wit that a complaint such as ours was no block to flourishing communication or happy living.

Our good mood got a big boost as a tall thin man stood up and pushing a curious small handcart with bits hanging off it, took his position up front, saying that his act was to proclaim a totally original dramatic soliloquy—an artistic Oulipopular fantasy that anybody in that room could grasp and proclaim. By now a warm mood was filling our gloomy lost waiting-room.

"My inspiration is Bard William and his famous play about a son of a Danish king who, on account of his Mum's disloyal actions following his Dad's assassination, is suicidal. Now, as many of you know, thanks to lots of inspiration and plain hard work in days past by various quixotic lipogrammarians, you can find good Ouliportrayals of this soliloquy in publication form (or by surfing on your PC), with artistic substitution of no-go words by words you and I can actually say.

"In passing, I must lift my hat to that giant of our "church"—I will call him Saint Adair—who did this just brilliantly in his translation of that grand Gallic classic—"A Void". (A warm round of clapping burst out at this salutation).

"As I am too proud just to mimic such past triumphs by simply doing a similar straightforward adaptation of this famous oration by incorporating words without that no-go sign, my wish was to concoct an art form that was truly original. My solution is to stop worrying about finding *words* as a substitution but to look at introducing *sounds*—using a particular sound for a particular sort of taboo word. I'll just ask you to think back to your grammar class at school.

"Look now at two things I brought along this morning: first, this audio contraption in front of you which I built in my back yard. It's no hi-fi but it's a magic box of tricks running on two forty volts with various knobs and buttons and playthings. And also study mindfully, if you would, this chart on my right:"

TABOO WORD With 5th sign	PROXY SOUND
A.) Noun	"drrring"
B.) Pronoun	"miaouw"
C.) Qualifying Word	"honk"
D.) Status or Action Word	"cuckoo"
F.) Modifying Word to D)	"woof-woof"
G.) Any Word not in prior list	"quack"

Occasional playful shouts of "Rubbish" or "I'm lost" or "Who's kidding who?" burst out all around. But our actor, unflinching, was sticking to his guns.

"No, just hold on and try to follow to my conclusion. My act is logical and straightforward and works in this way: If a noun in what I am about to proclaim contains that fatal symbol and so I cannot say it out loud, I'll push this black button for a sound of a ring on a door. That's for a noun. If it is a no-go pronoun, I'll play a cat's miaow. If I hit upon a rascal word that would normally qualify a noun, my input will consist of squashing this soft round ball on this horn in this way ("honk").

"For a "bad" word communicating action or status (viz: "go" or "is") I will just pull this switch to obtain a cuckoo's call. I trust I'm not losing you . . ."

"Hurry up!", "Go on with it", "I'm totally lost, chum!" Shouts and loud guffaws from a joking bunch in our back row.

"Finally two things I must just add, and that will finish things for good. If it's a non-U word with a function of modifying an action word (such as "quickly"), I will avoid saying it by playing a dog's bark on my apparatus. For any additional sort of "lipogramputational" word—shall I call it?—not found so far in prior classifications, I'll just fill in with a cry of a duck. So off I go . . . ."

Frowning and looking downcast, occasionally throwing his arms about, our actor put on a highly dramatic imitation of David Garrick or of that star of Victorian acting tradition, Irving, whilst manipulating his amazing apparatus. His clarity of diction and stunning histrionics would, without a shadow of a doubt, win wild plaudits at Stratford and (who knows?) might just obtain a nod and a wink from our Bard, looking down smiling from on high . . .

"To *cuckoo* or not to *cuckoo* that is *quack drrring* . . ."

As our star turn was launching thus into his most unusual word and sound show, a hush ran around our auditorium. Watching him in fascination mouthing occasional words, whilst dashing backwards and forwards to his sound box, all of us sat puzzling. Was all this tragic or comic? Should you shut up and show him profound admiration for such artistic passion and originality in his war against his affliction? Or should you vocally hail this original approach as a witty and frivolous way of short-circuiting our common malady and start joking along with him about his amazing imagination with a good long communal laugh?

Quack 'tis *honk* in *quack* mind to *cuckoo*
Quack slings and arrows of *honk drrring*.
Or to *cuckoo* arms against a *drrring* of *drrring*
And by opposing *cuckoo miaow*

Soon, holding back was an impossibility for us all. Throughout our rows of chairs, smiling was giving way to chuckling, giggling to guffaws and constant chortling. And our actor was showing satisfaction in our abundant mirth.

To *cuckoo*, to *cuckoo*
No *woof woof* and by a *drrring* to say *miaow cuckoo*
Quack drrring and *quack* thousand natural shocks
That *drrring* is *drrring* to. 'Tis a consummation
Woof-woof to *cuckoo cuckoo*

How can this man carry on with his histrionics, providing a sound if any word contains "that sign" and pushing a fitting button, if it's noun or pronoun or what you will? Amazing!

To *cuckoo,* to *cuckoo*—

To *cuckoo-woof-woof* to *cuckoo*: ay *woof-woof* is *quack* rub,

For in that *drrring* of *drrring* what *drrring* may *cuckoo*
Woof-woof miaow cuckoo cuckoo off this mortal coil
Must *cuckoo* us *drrring*.

By now all in our room had stood up, howling with joy and applauding wildly.

Woof-woof is *quack drrring*
That *cuckoo* calamity of so long *drrring*
For who would *cuckoo quack* whips and scorns of *drrring*,

Quack drrring wrong, *quack* proud man's *drrring*
Quack pangs of *honk drrring, quack* law's *drrring*,
Quack drrring of *drrring* and *quack* spurns
That *honk drrring* of *quack* unworthy *cuckoo*,
Woof-woof miaow miaow might his *drrring cuckoo*
With a *honk drrring*? . . . .

With a dramatic flourish, our actor flung his arms out, constantly taking many low bows in thanks for such a tumultuous ovation and wiping his hot damp brow with a tartan scarf.

VII

It is morning again as I start faithfully writing this continuation of my autobiography for Doctor Smith. But today my mood is bright, my spirits unusually high and my mind full of practical thoughts about coping with my infirmity and moving as rapidly as I can to a sort of normality.

My first contact with Oulipo, in fact all throughout that stimulating day in that most unstimulating location, Clapham Junction, was manna to my soul. I had quickly found common ground and good companionship with a host of warm trustworthy folks from around our world who had a similar complaint, and I got a myriad of tips and solutions and was told many a tall story on how to by-pass all sorts of difficulty in communication and win through brilliantly.

Thus I am proud to say that I am forthwith a paid-up participant of that shadow organisation Oulipoholics Anonymous—and am sworn by oath to start shrouding my condition from "ordinary" mankind, in addition to hiding my links with that judicious organisation. From now on, I must try not to stay dumb but to maintain a cautious sangfroid in my contacts with normal humans by optimising my patchy "fifth columnist" vocabulary, but using it sparingly. "Making do with my own company". That is a good way to sum up my total philosophy. But if on any occasion I am lucky to actually bump into a companion oulipoholic, I must show warmth and cordiality and aim to chat abundantly on any topic in any way I can.

In fact I am looking forward now to any forthcoming contact that might occur with any inhabitant of our world oulipopulation, through any oulipossibility which this might afford to oulipolish up my vocabulary, or to oulipour out my ouliposition on world oulipolitics—in particular with any important oulipolitician. What joy I would sustain if I, who am at this instant without any paid work, could obtain an ouliposition in a lipogrammar school? (I was told in Clapham that a pilot foundation with this sort of construct was now running in Canada).

But I must not carry on wasting hours in this foolish happy-go-lucky rumination. Obtaining a paid position in a London suburb not too far away is without a doubt my top priority this morning. So I finish my good strong Mocha, two portions of toast (with a thin lubrication of a soft fatty sunny product brought about by churning cow's milk!) and four spoonfuls of plum jam. And I go to pick up from my front doormat today's copy of our local *South London Clarion* and run through its "Situations Vacant" listings.

It's not a particularly stimulating bit of journalism, but I buy it as a substitution for that ultra right-wing (nay fascist) *Standard* rag, with which I would not sully my hands on any account following its vitriolic outbursts against our prior Socialist mayor and its blatant support for that public school oaf who now has his job! (I must stop talking politics though and carry on with my transcript).

I was struck straightaway by its top story, broadcast in bold capitals all across its front: *Local councillor in six million pound prostitution scam*—with a big grainy photo of its grinning culprit staring out. What's this? Naughty goings-on, on high, in our upright law-abiding suburb? But I had no wish to dip into any scandal right now. I finally found, half way through, a copious display of ads for jobs and I painstakingly ran through its long list of propositions. Most did not attract at all. I could not stomach working in a shop or a factory. As for a position in a bar or a bistro—anything similar to Luigi's—no thank you, kind sir! Good pay was important but not in any way as much as job satisfaction.

Working out-of-doors was a good way to go, I was now thinking. No claustrophobia. A bracing, invigorating activity. A horticultural pursuit, if I could find it, why not? Also, in this sort of job, you would probably work mostly in isolation—with probably no obligation for communication with any human. With nobody around, I could just simply savour my own company all day long.

Also I had a fair grounding in plants and shrubs going back to my youth and particularly during my school holidays—thanks to my rich cousin Mark, who had a vast manor and grounds in Cornwall and who would insist on my coming down to work with his staff in his plantations, floral displays and orchards as part of our family vacation, thinking it was good for my soul. I was only too happy to do so.

Starting to ring around for information about various situations vacant, I had no luck at first with my calls, but as I was almost giving up, right down among various small ads I found my nirvana. It was a paragraph, put in by a not too distant municipal council, which was looking for staff to work in its parks and country locations. Normal working hours and no Saturdays or Sundays. Salary not lavish but satisfactory—and as it was all fairly local, I would not find I was paying high transport costs.

Straightaway I put in a call and found it all plain sailing. A bright sounding young lady ran warmly through a short list of points, asking about my background, skills and know-how and giving a full indication of what pay and conditions would apply. I was happy with all this, asking how soon I could start, and hardly anticipating such a rapid invitation, thanks to a worrying lack of staff, I was told: "As soon as you can. A vast backlog of work has built up. This morning if you so wish". Brilliant!

I'll stop writing at this point and mail this dispatch straightaway to my good doctor as I will probably find I am too busy from now on to do so, on a daily basis . . . .

VIII

A quick look at a London Transport map had shown that I was in no obligation to go by car to start my forthcoming horticultural job. Crossing town all that way by 34 bus to that council HQ was in fact a propitious option and I saw that I could actually start my trip from a handy stop not fifty yards away from my front door.

I did not wait long for this bus to turn up. Jumping on board, I found that I was automatically stomping upstairs as I always did long, long ago during my infant school days, hoping that auspicious spot in its front row on top was vacant—and it was!—providing thus a broad panorama for watching all that was going on in and around our part of London, always so busy and fascinating. In fact, I had not brought a book or my daily Guardian to dip into on this occasion. I thought I would just wallow in a study of all that daily humdrum suburban activity. It's not surprising that visitors from abroad always savour occupying this position high up in a bus for watching that constant flow of amusing, curious habits or surprising activity among our capital city's inhabitants, and writing about it all on postcards to mail off back to family.

Traffic was habitually fairly solid in our particular district at this hour but this sluggish crawl along was providing a big opportunity to catch up on any particular innovations in its buildings, shops or parkland as I was passing by. I was soon looking out across a broad vista of lush grassy common ground with its tall oaks all around and this was slowly giving way to an untidy built up horizon. Soon I found I was in a shabby working class locality and our bus was hardly moving at all.

Our horizon was now an amalgam of grubby blocks of flats all of which could do with a thorough wash down. Also grim back-to-back rows of Victorian housing, windows and doors missing (possibly squats by now?), narrow untidy roads—half bricks, cast away cans and scraps of rubbish lying all around, rusty old cars with various bits missing, an odd stray cat or dog hobbling along or a young immigrant kid in a hood, kicking a tin can in front of him.

In contrast, two roads distant, I caught sight of a charming display to light up all that gloom: a big happy good-looking black family all smart in suits, colourful silk shirts and formal hats, including many old folks, twin baby boys in a pram and four young girls, big pink bows in all that mass of shiny curly hair, grinning and proudly walking in a column—off to church for nuptials, I was imagining. Following this joyous group, back all of forty yards or so, I also saw a colourful band of musicians playing joyously in unison on an unusual array of horns, tubas, piccolos, violins, violas, marimbas and cymbals. No angry Brixton riots to worry about on this patch.

Our bus was by now static with its motor shut off. I soon was conscious of many of us on board standing up, cursing and starting to alight. Information was soon broadcast to all still sitting down, that our road was now totally shut about sixty yards in front. British Gas, having found a substantial crack in a major mains running across this portion of tarmac, had built a cordon all around its location, and was busy drilling and digging down to put things right. It could, it was said, all last two hours.

What was to occur following this damning information was truly amazing. That man driving us, with our survival in his hands, (I'll just call him "busman" from now on), was obviously having a gigantic tantrum. Unhappy to wait hours in his small cab for that gang to finish what could turn out a long and tricky job, busman quickly did a staccato four point turn (a bus is long!), and shot off down a gap on our right into a labyrinth of narrow suburban roads. And with no bus stops to worry about, his foot was flat on his floor. All of us had no option but to hang on and simply pray.

For comfort in facing up to all this hair-raising bravado, I took out my walkman and put in a compilation of sonatas by Igor Stravinsky and an array of Paraguayan folk songs on a CD which I always carry around as in such traumatic situations it calms my mind totally. As that magical music was blocking out any sound from without and I had shut my lids from that midday sun, I was not particularly conscious of what was about to hit us.

Busman was by now losing his cool totally, grinding to a halt again in front of an additional roadblock. His solution was to roar backwards—at thirty, forty, fifty mph—up this particularly narrow road, miraculously avoiding by a maximum of a foot, twin rows of cars and vans all along his way. I was now watching it all in horror.

Again an abrupt right turn and our bus was moving swiftly along a broad downhill run. Focussing in a panic on all that was in front of us, I saw a viaduct looming up about thirty yards distant with a low horizontal iron archway across our path. Unfamiliar with this particular suburb and imagining busman was *au fait* with its topology, to think that this archway might turn out so low as to actually stop a tall bus (such as ours) in its tracks was far from my mind. In fact that is just what was about to occur.

Without warning a mighty thud shook us all. But our bus was not about to stop or slow down for such a minor glitch. It was continuing on its way forward and that razor-sharp rim of that viaduct was actually slicing off our roof backwards, making a frightful din similar to a circular saw, lifting it all away, yard by yard, as if it was a lid from a tin of pilchards, and curling it back into a tight roll which finally hung downwards, bouncing around at our back. In contrast to all that warm stuffy air upstairs, a sharp full frontal gust of wind was now driving strongly through our hair and forcing us to duck down or put up our hands and hold tightly on to our hats—or locks.

I was put in mind of that traditional sort of Victorian omnibus (with no roof) in which hardy commuting folk would wittingly climb up on top for an invigorating windy trip and watch all that was going on around and I was just smiling at this farcical situation. But I found that I was in a distinct minority: although it was not total panic up on top, I could catch sounds of gasps, shouts, howls of anguish, crying, grumbling, praying, to say nothing of a bout of manic laughing from a poor soul not far away.

Busman finally did stop, as a squad car with flashing lights was approaching. To avoid any implication in what was now a highly tortuous situation, most of us on board got off swiftly. Taking stock of this location, only a half-hour walk now from my goal, my local council HQ, I thought I would just carry on by foot. But first I put in a quick call to warn my forthcoming boss about my holdup. In particular, I had to vanish swiftly and so avoid any onslaught by that usual appalling bunch of cynical crusading British journalists, bound to turn up soon, all subscribing to that cynical motto: "Don't on any account allow truth to obstruct a good story".

IX

"Good to know you, Paul. Still got your hair on?"

"With such a ghastly fright, I thought you would turn up today totally bald!"

"No, just with snowy locks"

My final arrival around noon at that substantial Victorian mansion, now HQ for this municipal parks and public grounds organisation, was (to put it mildly) tumultuous.

Making my way into that spacious building and following arrows pointing up two flights of stairs to an information unit, I found all thirty or so outdoor staff sitting in a bright common room, going through a man-by-man (or I should say a man-by-woman) fortnightly work plan with a dynamic young lady who was chairing and tightly controlling a vigorous discussion.

As I slid bashfully in, loud shouts, chuckling and chortling burst out and many participants stood up to applaud, call out witticisms or simply put a hand out to grasp my own in a flood of sympathy and good humour. Virtually all my forthcoming work companions, I was told, had had an opportunity about half an hour back, to watch on TV in this room a dramatic broadcast, full of accounts from sobbing participants, all about my wayward bus and how it wound up sustaining that ghastly amputation in dark suburbia. In fact following my call to warn of my tardy arrival, our boss had told all and sundry that an additional staff assistant who was about to start work that day was in fact on board and up on top!

Virginia Mackintosh, for that was how our principal was known, was most cordial, coming up and shaking my hand warmly, but quickly turning back to that group to draw discussion to a finish. As soon as our room was vacant, Virginia said "How about our carrying on a discussion about your background and what you could start contributing to us all, upstairs in my study? It's got a broad panorama looking across all our grounds?" What could I say back but "Most willingly"?

Virginia was a short stylish woman of about thirty, looking chic in a smartly cut light brown suit, with long blond hair caught up in a pony tail. Running firstly through my CV and scrutinising my familiarity with a long list of horticultural topics (to which in fact I stood up satisfactorily, I am glad to say), I got confirmation of my pay and conditions and also my holiday quota.

Following my approval of such satisfactory provisions, I was told a fascinating history of this building and its grounds. It was run by its local council and was financially sound, thanks to a substantial ongoing annual grant from an anonymous local big-wig from his vast profits from trading in cotton.

Pointing to two big O.S. maps hanging across a back wall, Virginia took pains to clarify how our domain was laid out—its parkland, woodland (particularly its many oaks but also various softwoods), its vast planting plots, glass buildings, ponds, paths, public accommodation such as shops, snack bars, a futuristic auditorium, information points, first aid stations, lost and found huts (for kids and also kit!), plus a host of distinct planting subdivisions along all main paths throughout our domain.

"I trust you find that batch of mug shots hanging up on your right inspiring", Virginia was moving us along. "Our staff shot all of that pictorial display on show in front of us. With our squad, I run a monthly award for two topical and alluring photos of our parkland. In fact most of my gang carry around all day small digital apparatus for taking rapid instant snapshots."

Virginia took a long sip from a can of soft drink as I was now studying that array of portraits of my forthcoming companions (all looking happy and smiling—a good sign to anybody joining!) only to carry on with a rundown on staff policy:

"I think I ought to clarify my position. To do so, I must go back to my arrival thirty months or so ago. I took on a dying organisation, virtually bankrupt, with no action plan and no vision, a laid-back and constantly changing staff, who had no motivation (apart from a wrong sort), in fact constant militant tactics from stroppy unionists, still drawing inspiration from Moscow.

"So in my first annual plan, I had to focus on day-to-day survival and on putting our financial situation on a sound basis. I sold a radical approach to our Board—a short and a long duration action plan and on that basis got a substantial grant from our municipal council and also from various groups among local industry. I also found I was tapping into a strong body of opinion in favour of our making a substantial contribution to local tourism by building up and promoting, particularly to visitors from abroad, a major outdoor attraction.

"Staffing, as I just said, was simply all about starting from scratch and I took a major risk by sacking—or as I should call it, allowing to go—most of my quasi-communist payroll.

"What sort of horticultural staff should I look out for as a substitution? I thought long and hard and gradually hit upon a dramatic and daring solution: I was taking on historic parkland, with thousands and thousands of plants from all points of our compass and in no way simply from Britain—built up initially by a dynamic colonial family with a truly global vision. But this sad plot was now calling for a totally original approach, full of innovation and so I thought it was crucial to adopt a similar global vision in looking for collaborators, whom I saw as young, dynamic, with a good grounding in horticultural pursuits, but particularly coming from all around our world.

"So of my basic staff of thirty two—both boys and girls whom you saw just now—I count only six from Britain (and that's including you—and also a Scot who just dons a kilt most days and so, if caught stooping low to root out unsightly plants, is monstrously popular among us girls!). Just look at that row of individual photos of our group on that far wall display and you must admit, this is UN Plaza! Four hail from Italy, two from Spain, four from Holland, also two from Australia, a Lithuanian, a Latvian, a Saudi Arabian, a Madagascan, also an Irish faction—two from Dublin and two from County Antrim, a Moroccan, an Albanian, a Finn, two Brazilians and just a solo Russian.

"That snapshot to your right shows our companion Jokki, who hails from Tilburg in South Holland—a skilful plantswoman, but also a fantastic sportswoman, in fact an Olympic canal skating champion who won gold in Nagano, Japan. To unwind, that dynamic lady also has a habit of going off skating backwards at top rapidity (if our big pond turns icy)! What's important for us, though, is that Jokki has that Dutch knack of knowing all that anybody could possibly know about tulips, or any sort of bulb, coming from an illustrious family of plant propagators. Jokki is only happy out of doors, particularly if it is raining, and now controls our bulb syllabus, promising to grow a big display of black tulips for us in our Spring plot, along that south bank of our pond.

"To Jokki's right, that's Paolo from Sicily. Prior to joining us, this young man's job was driving a gigantic truck full of various brands of fashion goods, such as Gucci, Prada and Armani, fortnightly from Bari down in South Italy right up to Hamburg and back again, full of pork, pils and pastry. A bit of an Adonis, tall, muscular, a glorious body with his shirt off, this good-looking young man was thoroughly happy doing his trips by taking on board young girls hitching lifts for company and for who knows what. Paolo has a passion for rough, tough work. Nobody amongst us can dig as fast as him and Paolo is continuously singing out loud—in fact until 2004, his background was La Scala in Milan, with an occasional part as a star in its chorus, having sung in Aida last May.

"But this Spring, Paolo had a draconian bout of laryngitis and was having growing difficulty in maintaining his vocal stamina, so had to withdraw from Vivaldi, Puccini and company and look for a job in which straining his vocal chords was far from obligatory. Paolo now has a loyal following among many of our visitors for giving impromptu gigs, sounding similar to Placido Domingo or Luciano Pavarotti, during his work around our parkland with many of his fans now asking for him to do an official show for charity, singing an array of familiar arias among our floral arrays. Our board is giving it thought, I am glad to say!

"Now that colour photo, two along, throws light on why I had to sign you up to join us quickly. It's Conchita, a charming young Spanish woman, a skilful and artistic horticulturalist and a good hardworking collaborator who knows what grows and it shows—and who was, prior to coming to Britain, working in a high ranking capacity in courtyards in that magical Alhambra in Granada. Full of that immortal Muslim spirit of harmonious logical plant display, Conchita was just outstanding. Until that girl was hit for six by grim tidings of a tragic loss of an aunt and two cousins in a car crash. Conchita shot back straightaway four days ago to Andalusia, sobbing in agony and saying that with such frightful family obligations as of now, coming back was not an option. So it was sadly "adios" to us all for good. All our group is in shock and with our workload, I must fill that gap illico—so now it's your turn!

"Finally, it is my policy always to put anybody starting with us with a staff "custodian", for a fortnight's induction, to show him all around our domain and to start that pupil off by working with him. This photo is of your guardian. Good looking, no? It's our own Russian tovarich, Dimitri, an authority on woodland and shrubs. That's about all. So now I am proposing you go to find a snack straightaway in our kiosk downstairs and that you look out for him at two thirty p.m. in front of our pagoda. Dimitri is working today not far from that spot. But do you wish to ask anything about all this?"

I was most happy with this warm introduction from such a dynamic lady, but l had a burning topic to broach:

"I am so glad to join you all and trust that I will do my job to your full satisfaction. But I am not in such a high class of horticulturists as all that staff smiling back at us from that wall. I may sound bold in saying so but

I found it astonishing, following such a short discussion only this morning, how quickly you took on my candidacy without any vacillation. Also, I'm just a bog standard British national—not from any colourful faraway land"

Virginia was smiling broadly now.

"Don't go hiding your light, Paul. You obviously know a lot about our occupation. But I will admit to you that, apart from your skills, what was also marking you out in my mind for our vacancy during our introductory chat was your fascinating way of talking. Slow and cautious with a distinctly unusual approach to choosing vocabulary and syntax. Although you claim your nationality is British, I must say that I doubt it. But I am not asking you to show your passport and anyway I do not find it worrying. Your way of picking on words is just intriguingly worlds apart—and I go for such collaborators as, in my book, anybody who falls into a "worlds apart" group has broad horizons".

X

I had no difficulty in picking out Dimitri who was waiting stoically in front of our pagoda. Not only on account of his striking black track suit which was a standard work outfit bought from Paul Smith and worn by us all on duty in our parkland, but also as our Russian was so tall. Dimitri was in fact soaring a good foot and a half atop an abundant group of visitors from Thailand, all crowding noisily around its portal and consulting maps or handouts about our domain.

With Dimitri not noticing my various hand signals as I was approaching, it was not until I was finally standing just right in front of him, that my guardian for that day was *au courant* with my arrival. This giant of a man put a foot forward in a slightly military fashion and shook my hand firmly. It was an unusually formal salutation but as I quickly found out, Dimitri was no ultra socialising Latin and his grasp of our idiom was scanty—in short an upright thoughtful man of a minimum of words—and his disposition was inward-looking but gracious. I quickly got to know him and to think highly of him as a worthy companion.

"Found you at last!" said our Cossack with a warm grin, starting communicating in what I soon found was constantly short on words:

"My big tour starts now. You follow, thanks. This map for you to find layout of attractions." Just my amazing good luck, I was musing. Dimitri and I will work admirably in unison on account of our similar minimalist way of articulating.

So I was most happy just to stay taciturn and follow him on this painstaking circuit throughout our imposing park that day. In so doing, my main task was to try to imprint on my mind a distinct map of our domain's layout. Moving away from a growing crowd of bustling visitors in this hub of activity, our introductory walk had us strolling southwards down a broad path and through a chain of idyllic and colourful natural attractions, starting with a dazzling Spring display of magnolias—particularly magniflora—and also garlands of dogwood (cornus), laburnum and davidia. Forging onwards via a striking tall archway of distinct sorts of ivy, Dimitri took us through into a most artistic display of box topiary containing dramatic pyramids, spirals, big round balls, animals (such as dragons, stags, cats and stallions) and birds. Also past an amusing giant horizontal clock built up from various plantings, with in its midst a crazy cuckoo which would jump hourly out of a door and do a frantic rumba to a musical sound track from a Cuban band. All of this was on show within a group of circular "rooms" with low divisions of holly, taxus and bay. Right in its midst, I also caught sight of a grand old traditional Victorian sundial, an idyllic focal point on this bright sunny day.

Guiding us slowly around, Dimitri did not do much talking, but was signalling any particularly curious or artistic building or plant display along our path. My instructor would point to our spot on his map, or abruptly say occasional groups of words, stating approval or disapproval or making a short monosyllabic clarification or two.

"Much work to paint that" or "I dug this part" or "that planting is rubbish". It was as if my tutor had, word for word, my own vocal affliction. And as I could always talk back in similar shorthand, I was jubilant.

Going fifty yards onwards our path took us in front of a dwarf Palladian mansion—a sort of childhood folly—around which ran broad tracts of thousands of vibrant Spring bulbs. You could not stop admiring such a mind-boggling floral paint box tightly full of tulips, daffodils (in fact forty or fifty sorts of narcissus) in dramatic bursts of colour, running upwards towards a far horizon.

Diagonally across, balancing this small classical habitat and with crisply cut lawns all around it, I caught sight of a small workman's villa, all smart with its bright glossy paintwork—possibly an Arts and Crafts inspiration. I do not know why, but as I stood gazing at it, I found I was thinking of Victorian country folk and that romantic story by Thomas Hardy, as it did look far from any madding crowd.

"That building brought on back of lorry all way from Bridport." A typical handy input from Dimitri. Obviously I ought to commit such data to mind for, who knows, I might find I am told to run a tour on an odd occasion and should absorb all this background!

It was our turn now to pass by various classical horticultural displays, mirroring such gurus as Sir John Vanbrugh and "Capability" Brown. I soon found I was following a trail of "national" layouts, all containing a mass of individual plantings from a particular country and all combining formal inspiration and fantasy.

Dimitri took pains to point out his particular fancy—displays from China, Japan, Morocco and, surprisingly, also Scotland. I took a particular liking to a most unusual display from Colombia—a Mayan plantation of papaya, avocado, sapodilla, squash, pumpkin and chillis. A curious amalgam, not much to look at just now, but most outlandish. (I must also add that following thorough scrutiny, I did not spot that it had (or hid) any marijuana, coca or similar drug in cultivation—probably no bad thing!)

Our path was continuing to wind southwards, passing by rolling hills to our right. A broad South Downs panorama in fact, with skylarks soaring and chirruping, way up high in our sky. By now I was conscious of just how vast our total holding was. Although a constant flow of visitors was drifting throughout our domain, you could still find many vacant spots—totally calm, in which you could savour all that bird song or just nothing but a haunting air of tranquillity. What a utopia! And I am actually paid to work in this Arcadia?! I said this in fact to Dimitri and got a warm broad grin.

On making our way back towards our HQ at around four o'clock on a path winding through patchy woodland, both of us stood still in admiration at abundant displays of vigorous climbing plants such as wistaria and codonopsis. Thirty yards on, it was our turn to pass by a pair of old north-facing walls, giving us an opportunity for an assiduous look at a host of vigorous shrubs such as pyracantha, viburnum and forsythia, sprouting among partly crumbling bricks.

Although this long walk was a total joy, I was now worn out by all that I had to absorb and I was dying for that mobility buggy of ours to turn up impromptu and carry us both back to HQ. But, no such luck! Notwithstanding,

I was walking back through to our Main Building in high spirits. Dimitri's tour took us about two and a half hours in all and I had had so much to absorb. I was also musing as to why, with my partiality for outdoor pursuits, I had hardly known about this Arcadia in my youth. No doubt it had to do with its ruinous condition and abandon prior to Virginia's arrival.

But abruptly I was hit by a most unusual sight, a vivid flash back to my past. It was an old London tramcar on display in a child's playground. Its upstairs had no roof (just don't bring that back to my mind!) and it had no window downstairs at its front, so its driving position was outdoors and it had a circular stick for manipulating by a workman to pilot it along its tracks. I saw two small boys fighting for a turn at driving it. A captivating plaything for a child to actually touch, in comparison with that mass of transitory sooty trains at Clapham Junction.

Slowly a flashback was filling my mind—a visit I had to this domain long ago as a small child with my old aunt Matilda, not now of this world—God guard that lady's soul! I had actually had a go at driving this contraption in that distant part of my happy boyhood, romanticising in my mind about having a grown-up job as such an important man standing upright in front and proudly guiding this giant antiquity along, basking in all that admiration coming from all that good folk on board.

Dimitri was watching and smiling, as my vision was vanishing.

"You too big to go on that. But that is all for you today. You study map and park layout.

Until Monday—hard work for us both".

Adding in his own idiom: *"Da svidanya. Bolshoi sad, mnogo raboti."*

XI

A Saturday morning is to my mind just right for tarrying an hour or two on my divan, horizontal and in total inactivity, dozing and savouring all that outstanding warmth within my quilt. But that was too optimistic as I was abruptly struck by a sharp ringing sound on that auditory apparatus you pick up for distant two-way chit chat. (All right, I grant you that as a fully paid-up Oulipolyglot, it should amount to child's play to find a fitting analogy or apt colloquialism to portray in my tight vocabulary that obligatory domiciliary contraption. But I am still only half conscious!) Fumbling around irritably in that half dark, I finally put my hand on it.

"Good morning, Paul. It's Doctor Smith. I trust you will pardon this call but I thought it was fitting by now to avoid my PC and in fact to ring you to catch up and discuss things by word of mouth. But first I do want to say bravo for forwarding daily accounts in writing of all your activity. All show both an outstanding lift in your communication ability and also how you start coping with various additional ups and downs—such as your u-turn in jobs and your visit to Clapham Junction. Congratulations! And do carry on mailing your tidings to us—though by now with no obligation to do so on a daily basis. Just post off occasionally a summary of anything significant that occurs.

"My contacts in Oulipo, following its railway station symposium, told us all in our Slough consultancy about how warmly our group took in your cordial participation in that rally. Things do look promising for you. Bravo too for your horticultural opportunity. I trust I am not wrong in sounding optimistic about your condition."

I was in point of fact most happy with this call and said so, adding that I was coping admirably.

"Thanks for calling, Doctor Smith. I do think I am slowly improving my basic communication with ordinary folk but what I find worrying is how things will pan out in this outdoor job which I am just starting. I must try to play my full part amongst a band of smart young collaborators who know botany backwards and will not, I think, put up with fools gladly. I firmly maintain that my basic know-how and skill in working with plants and planting is satisfactory, but how can I know if that's right? A good point is that most of our group do not hail from this country, so will most probably commit habitual *faux pas* in pronunciation and vocabulary—just as I do. Good common ground for bonding. But as a local, I must avoid looking an ignoramus and a laughing stock on account of my occasional funny way with words.

"My major worry is my critical inability in coping with colours, crucial in any floral discussion. I could not possibly talk my way through a rainbow. What I can say is not to much avail. You would not find all that many black, brown or pink blossoms or blooms around our park. So if I must distinguish this cultivar from that cultivar by naming its particular colour, how do I say it without using that mournful sign? Is it a crimson poppy or a pillar box poppy or a cardinal poppy or a snowy or a milky or a chalky poppy?

"Do I call various tulips sunny or saffron or go about naming contrasting blooms as cadmium or, God forbid, "as vivid as a dark plum"? Also if anything is similar in colour to grass, may I say "chlorophyll" to portray it? As a highbrow horticulturalist, could I in fact claim to own chlorophyll digits? Or do I simply inform all and sundry that I am colour blind? My compass can only point to north and south. I can always go forwards and backwards and also turn right but cannot say I am on my way towards its opposing compass point . . . ."

Doctor Smith was chuckling warmly as I was waxing lyrical, hoping to attract sympathy about my handicap.

"Look, Paul, it's normal for you to display this sort of misgiving about failing to gossip and looking foolish in company. But you did point out to us, in a daily summary of yours, that you will usually pass much of your day in your parkland in a solitary situation and so you can stay fairly dumb throughout. In fact what is just as important, if I may say so, is finding topics having nothing to do with such horticultural pursuits, that you can chat and laugh about.

"Also do maintain your habit of writing down and assimilating, day-by-day, all your valid lists of unknown compliant words for using to prompt colloquy on an array of topics. Go out and buy a big Oxford dictionary and pass an hour or two daily with it, tracking down unfamiliar and atypical nouns and so on. All copious ammunition, so that in any profound discussion that might occur, you will not stand out as an ignorant bumpkin, but as a studious, almost donnish scholar. Building up your rich hoard of unusual and striking vocabulary can assist you in scoring points against anybody criticising you for a poor grasp of your diction and phrasing."

"That sounds worth a try", I thought as our talk was finishing and Doctor Smith was proposing to call again in a fortnight.

Around midday, I did go out to top up on food and drink and, with my doctor's sound words in my mind, I also paid a visit to my usual bookshop, coming back panting with a colossal dictionary. I sat down to dip into it straightaway. I had in past days habitually put down in writing, on a thick batch of blank cards, a gargantuan potpourri of valid words on a host of multifarious topics which I thought worthy of storing in my mind. But dipping now into my outstanding acquisition with its prodigious vocabulary, I found that I could quickly commit to mind truly unusual finds, including many "good" words originating in distant parts of our world—in fact from lands in which so many of our horticultural staff had roots.

Good Lord, just look at this curiosity—*ailurophobia*—"having an unnatural fright of cats"—brilliant! I'm not ailurophobic at all. Am I, Monty? Or this word—*horripilation*—"with your hair standing upright"—and how about this? *Panurgic*—"fit to do anything". I must add all this to my hoard. What an amazing book this is!

I was continuing for hours to draw up and absorb this fascinating list off pat, labouring past nightfall and again for most of that following day. Thus by Monday morning as I was going to work on a bus (downstairs on this occasion, not surprisingly!), my mind was numb with what you might call a painful bout of glossary saturation. But I had a strong craving to try out as many of my additional unorthodox articulations as I could on any sort of individual looking for a chat on board this public transport.

I soon thought I was lucky as a short smart lady of about sixty with a capacious handbag, wiping raindrops from a wrinkly brow, sat down on my right, looking my way and obviously longing to talk about things.

"What a ghastly day, isn't it? And it was said on Radio Two just now that this downpour would last right through till tonight."

It was not too inspiring a discussion gambit to start with but I had to stay civil.

"No doubt about it, Madam. It's a big storm."

"And tomorrow will turn out truly cold, thanks to that sharp North wind which is blowing up."

"Most probably".

By now, I could not think of anything worth saying but this lady was in full oratory.

"Just so. But in two days, I'm told, it will turn out mild and fairly sunny. So I can wash all my windows"

What could I find to say back? No doubt if I was just taciturn, this prattling might grind to a halt. But, no such luck.

"I'm downright poorly, you know. Coughs, colds, sciatica, arthritis. I'm an invalid, always at my doctor's. His waiting room is full of old folk looking awful. Do you find it that way? I just can't stop blaming such awful downpours on all this global warming. And it's so cold too. Wouldn't you say so?"

A rising mood of irritation was building up in my mind. This was not what I was anticipating as a warm up talk prior to my arrival at work. I was hoping for an opportunity for a stimulating discussion in which I could try out all my sparkling additional vocabulary. But it did act as a prompt to try out my status as a first class wordsmith, in particular by using as much as I could of that unfamiliar donnish vocabulary I had just dug up in my gigantic dictionary. Turning back to that poor garrulous soul, I said:

"I concur, Madam, that it is rawky today and that sky looks fuscous. I won't mamaguy you and I can't go in for catoptromancy, but I doubt that it will turn out a coruscant day."

A blank look of horror was now clouding this loquacious lady's pallid physiognomy. Standing straight up angrily and backing quickly away four rows from my spot in our bus, this good soul was starting to shout. All on board sat smiling broadly or just watching in confusion as to how this situation would unfold.

"What a disgusting way to talk to an old lady. Such vulgar words! Quick, call Scotland Yard! Out of your mind, that's you. Sick!"

Gradually, faint contagious chuckling among all on board that public transport was transforming into chortling, and soon into loud hilarity. And by now, I was in full ranting flight, triumphant in my ability to put across such unfamiliar articulation.

"Sick? I am a touch atrabilious this morning with a fugacious splanchnic condition as I had a vagarious night. I am a bit of a noctambulist too. I cannot say that I am sick but I abhor sitting on this omnibus as it can bring on an attack of ochlophobia. Notwithstanding I find this particular situation nothing but floccinaucinihilipilification!"

A tumultuous bout of clapping burst out at my oratory as that poor garrulous woman, in total shock now, ran back to jump off. I did not mind if this commuting crowd found I was unkind or slightly ridiculous. I was proving that I could vastly amplify my vocabulary.

But I was also thinking: how is it that curious things almost *always* occur on any occasion I am using public transport? Difficult to avoid and I cannot just walk to work, now can I?

XII

Arriving to start work at our park HQ with half an hour in hand on this my first morning, my instant action was to go to find out what both Dimitri and I had as a job plan for today. For this sort of data, all that our staff had to do was to log in and consult on a daily basis a giant plasma display unit in our main hallway and to run through and download individual work status lists with locations, timing goals and tool allocation. Virginia's organisational ability was just amazing.

Punching in my password and clicking on my icon, I saw that I was to accompany Dimitri and work this coming day in division D32 South of our parkland. Our first job was building an additional floral plot, involving digging soil and mulching, planting rows of spring blooms, and giving grass a good haircut. This was to occupy us for four days. Our display also had information on today's local climatic conditions, mild with a light South wind and a mix of sun and cloud, but with a possibility of light rain around two p.m.

As I still had a fair wait prior to starting work, I thought I would carry on scrutinising that vast bank of information at a touch of a button and find out about our global action plan for all staff throughout our parkland during forthcoming months. In an instant, it was all fully laid out.

For our final days in April I saw among our tasks—mowing lawns, planting up carnations and pinks, lots of composting, putting in dahlias, and adding supports. Also sowing a last batch of hardy and half-hardy annuals and a final planting of bulbs, notably gladioli. Our fruit orchard was also down for spraying with ammonia. Finally, maintaining paths and tidying fountains was on that list.

Our on-going diary had plans for continuous pruning of our bountiful stock of shrubs, initial clipping of our topiary, pinching out growing tips of vigorous plants, staking of tall blooms and a proposal for us to start planting out an abundant colourful hardy annual display in start-up plots right by our shops, containing candytuft, choisya, clarkia, linnaria, maroccana and linum grandiflorum.

But all was not plain sailing. Worrying clubroot in birch, walnut and willow was found right down south in our woodland and coping with it quickly was crucial. Also a high-priority task was fungi control. (A crisis "Plant First Aid Unit" was in formation among our staff for stamping out such ills).

In all, this was a simply fascinating navigation around our parkland's basic goals. Moving away from that display and bidding good day to my work companions, I was thinking back to why I had sought this kind of job—to avoid too much social contact by working solo on account of my vocal hang-up. It was obvious that collaborating in a duo or trio was normal for this particular organisation. But in this parkland, I was amazingly lucky. Virginia had in fact found my way of communicating fascinating, if not totally British! Thus I had my boss on board. And with that idiosyncracy in common with Dimitri, my outlook was looking distinctly rosy.

I found D at our plot for today, sitting on a low wall, plunging a soup spoon into a giant pot of probiotic apricot and vanilla yoghourt and occasionally taking big gulps of piping hot *Rooibos* from a giant mug vaunting an inscription "A gift from Happy Blackpool". I was to find out that Dimitri drank six ominously strong cups of this forbidding liquid throughout his working day. What I was also to fathom by and by was that a cryptic inclusion in this daily tonic was a stimulating slug of Smirnoff vodka. "To guard against icy winds coming all that way from Vladivostok", as my good Russian companion would proclaim.

As both of us dug into that day's work, small talk at first was scant. A callow tyro, I thought it politic to allow Dimitri to allot tasks among us both, following our joint action plan. Our taciturn collaboration swung swiftly into action, with an odd nod or wink or grin or hand signal. But gradually both had an inclination to start talking about our backgrounds in our tortuous ways and in that short first day, whilst sharing jobs, I was to pick up much of his sad biography.

His story was astonishing. Born into a shockingly poor family in Nijni Novgorod, an orphan by his 4th birthday and brought up by a tyrannical aunt, Dimitri was a bright scholar, winning a grant to study in a top Moscow institution and obtain training in—to put it bluntly—spying. His first major activity was in London as a "diplomat" living incognito in Finsbury Park and working in his consular division issuing visas to British tourists wishing to visit Russia. But in addition my companion was acting as an important spy—this was prior to Glasnost—focussing on Britain's anti-ballistic capability. This had him roaming constantly around our hills and stalking various military installations, posing as an ordinary local inhabitant simply taking his dog for a walk.

His total lack of fluidity in talking in any idiom was of no import to his work as Dimitri had a most singular and striking gift, an ability for assimilating totally (in fact photographically) and storing in his mind all that his vision could focus on and absorb, simply by glancing at a location—silos, IBMs, aircraft, buildings, military apparatus, any sort of dish. Back at HQ, at sundown, our "spy" could transmit such visuals from his brain to unambiguous hard copy, by writing and drawing, providing illustrations and words for his KGB contact who would call him, jokingly but in total admiration, "Kodak cranium". (So it was not surprising that upon gazing in a twinkling at Virginia's thorough point by point job summary for us both with its timings and manifold plant lists, Dimitri had it all succinctly in that skull of his for instant download day by day. Without asking, all I had to do was follow his tactics).

I should just finish his story. Dimitri was tiring of living in Britain in this way as an impostor, posing as an ordinary (if dumb) pub—and football-loving chap, supping pints in small country inns in common with locals, shouting his support for First Division football champions, watching soaps on ITV and Sky—a captivating way of living but in solitary limbo. So with communism fading and an obvious thaw in contacts with our capitalist world, Dimitri was to turn his back on his past and sought a way out as an official inhabitant of our island by applying for and obtaining British nationality. Or such was my conclusion!

As for gaining his daily crust in his country of adoption, our good Russian, following a similar logic to my own, was looking to avoid constant word of mouth contact with groups of individuals in any vast organisation, by taking up any sort of solo activity—such as an outdoor horticultural occupation. This was not a first occasion for Dimitri, as working on God's soil, particularly to grow food, was a throwback to his hungry days as a lad in his USSR.

Adopting a harmonious rhythm to our various tasks and savouring our mutual minimal approach to discussion (you could justifiably call it small talk!) our day was passing quickly. I did find I was, just occasionally, thinking back to my mortifying trauma at Luigi's which was far away now and thanking our Good Lord that I was rid of that disastrous charivari.

So Doctor Smith, as I sign off for today, I do firmly think that I am now at last on my way up.

XIII

Following your gratifying proposal, Doctor Smith, that I should stop aiming to dispatch to you a daily diary from now on, I am typing a short summary of my last four days' conduct. It's Friday night and I am in high spirits as I am finding that my job transformation, from that claustrophobic and doomsday Italian subjugation to an invigorating practical outdoor occupation, is nothing short of miraculous.

Working with Dimitri in our park is most gratifying. Though about fifty, my companion is young in spirit, has a commanding horticultural know-how and is a joy to accompany, with our having so much in common, particularly with both of us constantly juggling a minimalist vocabulary and joking in so doing. Our approach is to avoid too much trivial chat and to focus on any task in hand, although both of us do talk frankly about our own singular individual history and what in our past had brought us to finish up working in this particular parkland.

Among a long list of tasks occupying us in our past four days (all of which anybody could look up on our giant PC at HQ): marking out, digging up, building, mulching and planting six additional floral plots, following our own draft proposals, in focal positions in various parts of our grounds, pruning, and mowing lawns. Our total layout is all looking most promising—and as soon as buds burst out, it will without doubt win plaudits.

I am continuing to go to work and back by bus. Traffic along that labyrinth of roads is frightful and I would always find driving my car to and fro through constant jams arduous—particularly coming back, physically worn out. Whilst on this topic, I think it worth informing you of a spiritual hiatus that I had by missing my usual transport back to my flat today. Taking far too long to monitor my job allocation for this coming Monday, I got out of our grounds only to watch my bus rapidly moving away from our stop. Implying a half hour wait—which I did not look forward to with much gusto, as it was now starting to rain.

But a solution was at hand. Straight across that road I saw a small traditional parish church with its door ajar and I could just catch a soft haunting sound of an organ playing within. I cannot pass by such a building of worship without slipping into it for a short visit. It is a habit going back to my halcyon days as a choirboy in St Albans. Nowadays I cannot find much conviction about Christianity in my mind or soul on a daily basis, I am sorry to admit. But by just crossing that portal into a mansion of our Lord, and coming into contact again with its profoundly spiritual surroundings, I find my faith coming back in a warm consolatory flood—until, as I turn my back on it all by moving out again into our impious world, I automatically switch off and pick up my Doubting Thomas hat and put it on again.

Making my way in through that florid Victorian doorway, I saw that this church was void of humanity, apart from an organist sitting up high, abutting a rococo altar, out of this world in his vigorous playing of a potpourri of Bach. A strong round full sound was vibrating throughout its mock Gothic canopy and a mass of rich bass chords was rattling its windows. This musician was obviously practising and passing quickly from composition to composition. From my school days I maintain a fascination with classical music—principally for an organ, which I did play on occasions and I could pick out his various options. It was an amalgam of toccatas—from that all too familiar D Minor, to that constant up and down motif in Bach's F Major. Surprisingly this local virtuoso was focussing on toccatas and not continuing with any part two of such works, avoiding no doubt in his alacrity, any difficulty in coping with its contrapuntal intricacy.

I took a slow walk around this small mansion of God, admiring a host of abundant floral displays, four of which sat most dazzlingly on its high altar. But I did not catch sight of any good lady from that parish whom you usually find busily arranging such colourful attractions. Nor could I spot any sign of a vicar. I did stop to look at a charming baptismal font and to study a host of moving inscriptions on tombs of locals lost in both World Wars. In all, I was savouring a history of a typical suburban community with its highs and lows, its joys and sorrows.

Following a short gap, organ music (still by good old JSB—his Fantasia in G Minor) was filling that church again. This particular composition was to drown my spirit in poignant nostalgia. As a boy, I was always putting on an LP of this particular work to savour. I had visions flooding back from my childhood of all that magic of Midnight Mass and Christmas jubilation—of holly and ivy on our high altar, of gifts among our family, of singing carols (*In dulci jubilo* was my top option). Again I was longing for such long lost days. I sat down in a front row as that glorious playing was continuing to pour out and I found, most unusually, I had a compulsion to pray.

But how would my partial ability in manipulating vocabulary start coping nowadays with that primary act of worship—what I can only call "Our Lord's rogation" or "supplication"? I just had to try as hard as I could.

Our—I obviously cannot say "Dad" or "Papa". *Lord*—that will work, although it has lost an important admission of a family link.

Who art up in our sky. That will do, but it is not totally fitting.

"Thy ID is holy"—ID is a bit too worldly—how about simply using: *Thou art most holy*? It's succinct in comparison with *Holy is what all of us know you as*—and it's ungrammatical to switch from thou to you, anyway.

May thy kingdom hold sway.

May thy will know no bounds, down in this world as it will up in your sky. This is not so difficult!

Grant us today our daily—"loaf", that's too familiar—"food?" "provisions?". I think I ought to say: *victuals.*

> *And pardon us our sins*
> *As all of us pardon such as who sin against us*
> *But stop us from doing wrong*
> *For this is thy kingdom*
> *Thy might and thy glory*
> *Day and night*
> *Ad infinitum*

And how do I finish that incantation? That closing word of four signs is plaguing my brain. It contains our outlaw and I cannot think up a short homologous backup option.

May it all turn out satisfactorily—a sorry mouthful, is all I can track down!

During my bus trip back to my flat, I was continuing to turn my translation around in my mind, amid a dark mood of frustration about how poor a wordsmith I was proving. I would not stand out as particularly adroit to anybody from among our Oulipublic, whom I might bump into at Holy Communion!

So around midnight, with my mind still sprightly and with nothing worth watching on TV, I thought I might look again at that invocation—in particular at its first all important noun, signifying "a man with an affinity to his natural child". I would try to find out in how many idioms around our world this word was taboo for any "Fifth columnist" Christian and how difficult it would turn out for him to find synonyms for it in pronouncing this invocation to God.

On consulting this and that bi-lingual dictionary in my unassuming library, I saw that such a common word was a block throughout. I could not avoid that irritating symbol if I was formally translating "papa" into Latin, or into that classical vocabulary of Plato or Pythagoras, or into that idiom of Parisians or of Bavarians, or into Spanish, Italian, Russian or that lingo dominant in Portugal and Brazil. That stubborn villain of a sign was still found in all such local nouns. That said, as a final consolation I did root out that in Cardiff's original patois, its formal word for "dad" is simply *Tad*, in parts of Scotland you might find a transcription of it as *Ar n'Athair* and if you grasp basic Aramaic you could opt for *Abwoon d'bashmaya*.

I am now yawning—so I will call a halt and tomorrow possibly just hand this conundrum across to our savants in Oulipo to carry on looking for solutions. I quit. Good Night, all!

XIV

As my old Scottish Grandma Dorothy would habitually say long ago to us young cousins in a thick Glasgow intonation: "Don't you bairns count your poultry prior to its chicks starting to hatch". Although in making that point with a total ABC capability, my granny did not proclaim it strictly with this group of words!

Busily making up my picnic lunch for taking to work last Thursday morning I had a nagging worry on my mind. It was a strong conviction that I would again today find it difficult to concoct anything original about my work in any dispatch to Doctor Smith. This was in fact my fourth day of diarist's block.

In various accounts this past month, I had told my psychology consultant all that I could find to say about my linguistic capability and my job—about our dynamic administrator, our organisation, our parkland, its history, its layout, its floral displays, its buildings, our cosmopolitan staff, my good chum Dimitri and his shady past. I had, I thought, shown in all such accounts, a growing skill in communicating a host of goings-on straightforwardly and promptly. My vocabulary was growing day by day, as I was constantly looking for virgin words and phrasings. But what's original today, pussy cat?

To put it bluntly, my mind was numb and I was dumb. Could I simply limit my composition to putting down what

I was making for my lunch? Food is a thought-provoking topic to go to town about and it had not shown up as a topic in my submissions for many days. Would this trivial contribution do? "Today's picnic will consist of a brown loaf sandwich full of luscious thin cuts of Parma ham, tomato and chicory salad with a good coating of hot grainy mustard. Also a banana, a Kit-Kat bar and a can of sparkling H2O. (I don't go in for any sugary soft drinks. Nor any alcohol, if I'm at work!)."

But I could hardly call this 'world-ranking tidings'. I had to discard such banality and with no backup inspiration, to start out glumly towards my bus stop, whilst still wracking my brains for any original thought to put down in writing that particular night . . .

Sitting moodily on my usual public transport, I was not obviously privy to such an astonishing commotion as was to occur to both of us during our work in our woods from around midday that day, providing not only a fascinating story which I could impart to my doctor, but also which would radically transform both of our individual situations for good. It was a traumatic affair involving a historic hoard of gold coins, two squad cars from our local constabulary in an almighty crash, a wild fight with a raving bunch of journalists, our parkland closing to all visitors for a fortnight and D and I both out of a job and out of town.

I will just wind our clock back to my arrival at work two days ago. First, it was particularly important for us all to consult our individual job lists point by point on our visual display unit as our gallant principal was, unusually, away all day. Virginia had to go to London to pick up a major National Trust award for outstanding horticultural activity and to savour a first class lunch with various big wigs. All our staff had a plan to assign half an hour around four thirty p.m. that day to adorning Virginia's "control room" with balloons and bunting and various floral sprays. Jokki would cook and bring in a gigantic fruit tart with fairy lights and also many magnums of Jacquart Brut Tradition NV for a loyal toast to our champion, back with us at that point.

Dimitri and I had a vast four day task to accomplish in our woodland, right down by our park's south boundary. Originally a part of our job allocation for this coming May, our top botanist had brought forward plans for us to start tackling straightaway what was a major affliction of oak root fungal attack—a hazard to our public now as many a bough or big branch could fall down without warning. It was also part of a basic tidy-up in that locality. Both of us had a hard job to do, digging up or sawing down or uprooting ailing birch and willow and slicing back sick oaks and ash. In addition it was no comfort to find a surprisingly warm sun shining down on us, as soon as trunks and branch following branch had had a chop.

Support from additional park staff was constant—driving up on tractors or pulling carts and taking away vast mounds of sprigs and boughs as it was all cut away. Work was slow as much of our wood was old and clad in thick climbing plants—many worth saving.

Around noon, our calm world was to fall apart. Dimitri was slaving away, digging down and chopping at a big clump of roots and lifting out chunks of wood and clods of clay, whilst I was dumping all that rubbish into a cart. Abruptly a mighty roar sprang out from our Russian navvy as I saw him lift, not without difficulty, a curious box from a big cavity just dug out.

His find was a small oblong trunk, as old as hills and about a foot and a half across, built of wood but with a sort of animal skin casing full of splits and cracks all around it.

Grinning broadly, Dimitri took up his find in his arms and put it down slowly in front of us both. It had a rusty lock of sorts on its front, which Dimitri painstakingly took apart, to lift its lid cautiously upwards.

What both of us saw had us whistling in both shock and jubilation. Within that shabby box was a prodigious hoard of old gold coins, chains and rings, shining up at us. Dimitri, laughing madly, was dipping his hands into this glinting king's ransom and holding an array up to his chin, watching it all fall trickling through his digits and shouting. "Look, gold . . . *zoloto* . . . a gift of God . . . a jackpot, at last. I'm rolling in it! And you too! Just look at all this!" (D was taking up coin by coin, twisting it from front to back, focusing on kings' portraits and coats of arms.) "It contains florins, half-florins, crowns, ryals, farthings, groats, dinars and marks. A mountain of bullion, worth thousands and thousands." I was struck dumb, not just by this find, but also by Dimitri as such an authority on numismatics.

Nobody apart from us two was in our vicinity to watch all this animation at that particular instant. But my Russian conspirator was suspicious and took a rapid look all around, saying in a low murmur: "Quick. It's just us two right now. You and I must stash this all away from anybody from our gang who is bound to show up soon. This find is strictly ours. It will turn us both fabulously rich."

I found it awkward to say anything back in support of his claim as I was thinking that our parkland probably had rights apropos any long lost bullion which might turn up in this way and I said so. In Boy Scout fashion, all I could grunt was: "You do it, if you want to, Dimitri, but I can't join in. It's probably unlawful. But I will stay mum and not say a word about it."

Dimitri, laughing uproariously, was now hastily stuffing his prodigious find back down into its original cavity, piling soil on top and stamping down on it all.

At that instant, both of us saw two of our parkland companions arriving in a truck to pick up our cuttings and rubbish. Dimitri instantly took hold of a fork and turning his back was starting to attack a mass of roots in a contiguous clump of sick poplars, singing a lullaby, a good way away from his burial plot.

"Lots of shouting in this part of our woods" said Jimmy, our parkland's Australian navvy, a touch suspiciously. "Found anything unusual?"

"Not in this spot, chum. Just roots and shoots, sticky clay and bits of rock" Dimitri told him firmly. "But an instant ago, I got an SMS from my girl Barbara to say that I had just won a thousand pounds in our local hospital's grand tombola. So it's off to Brighton for us on Saturday for a saucy stay. Yum yum! That's what I was crowing about"

"Lucky individual" was kangaroo man's opinion, although not looking totally happy with that slightly suspicious account. With his cart now full, this unsought infiltrator got out of our way, driving his load slowly back towards HQ.

What to do from that point on? Dimitri had his own smart plan. It was for us to carry on labouring as normal in that distant part of our park until four thirty, as our work was to finish around that hour for Virginia's party. At that point, my companion would dig out his find, climb up our parkland back wall with it, jump down into a narrow country road which ran along our boundary, and find his paramour plus car waiting for him for a rapid withdrawal. I said I would act dumb, join our group for a glass of bubbly and not say a word to anybody about his find. To anybody asking why Dimitri had had to abscond, I would say our companion had a throbbing pain in a back tooth and was in town having it out.

I was awkward and anxious, split twixt loyalty towards my Russian companion who probably did warrant part of that bounty for finding it, but also with a misgiving that our parkland would find out all about it and claim its rights, putting us both (not just him) in a dubious position for such a blatant act of misappropriation. In short, I could not simply say I was in no way party to that shady act.

What I did not fathom at that instant was that a spotlight was now firmly on us both, thanks to a group of our parkland companions, spying on all our actions from afar. A rumour was starting to fly around our organisation that a man on our payroll had found a costly historic curio four foot down in our woodland. Our administration, without Virginia taking things in hand, had found it all a tall story—an annoying distraction at such a busy point in our workload and had thrown out any thought of following up on it, instructing all informants to avoid such distractions and go back on duty forthwith.

But what put a cat among that bunch of cooing birds was that this talk of our town did prompt a park assistant, hungry for a financial pay off, to contact a small tally of journalists who would probably find it a good story to look into. And so it was that at that climax of our working day, just as Dimitri was frantically digging down again into that all important spot for his stash, six staff from two lurid tabloids paid us a visit, taking flash photos and fighting for copy.

"Hi folks! I'm a Sun columnist. From Britain's top daily. You must talk to us. And only us. About all that lost gold and stuff. Do us that big favour and I'll warrant it will turn out worth it for you. Got it?"

"No, look this way. I'm from your Daily Mail, this country's paramount journal that all our population trusts. It will print a truthful account. Sign us up and you will profit."

Dimitri's irritation was obvious. "This story of lost gold is rubbish. All that was dug up at our lunch hour was a pair of old boots which I had to bury back. Sorry to disappoint you. Why don't you hacks just withdraw and all go back to your own individual factory of scandal and half truths?"

But that flock of outlandish paparazzi was not going to pull out willingly. Dimitri put a stop to his digging and striding right up to that group, said indignantly. "Look, you lousy bunch of propagators of lurid fiction, just grasp this plain fact, would you? This is simply a tidy up job in an ordinary calm bit of woodland. I did not find, nor will you find, any outstanding historic loot in or around this spot, so buzz off and say to Murdoch and all your top brass that this story of lost booty is total fiction".

Without warning, additional bursts of flash photography lit up our woodland. From that point, things got rapidly out of hand. By now, Dimitri was livid. In an instant my companion was hitting out with his fists among all that intruding group, drawing blood, smashing photo apparatus and causing this scribbling bunch to withdraw hotfoot.

Straightaway four hoots on a car horn rang out, a sign to Dimitri that his paramour Barbara was, according to plan, waiting for him in that narrow road backing on to our domain.

Prior to my saying "Jack Robinson", Dimitri had dug down into his original cavity, drawn out that historic box, pulling off its lid and saying: "Look Paul, my faithful pal, I must now run away for good and so you and I must say *da svidanya*. But I still want to split my find fifty-fifty with you. It's only fair and I find you a star. Go on. Dip in."

But I stood still, shaking my cranium vigorously. I was no crook. I could not join in.

"Thanks anyway, but no thanks . . . And good luck to you, old buddy" was all I could mouth. About to vanish, Dimitri shook my hand firmly, dropping into my palm a small handful of gold from his bountiful find. "Lucky charms for my kind *droog*. So you can always think of your horticultural chum. And with a giant hug, my companion was off . . . for good . . . or almost.

Stuffing his box of bullion way down into his anorak and zipping it up tightly, Dimitri was bounding upwards to grasp thick strands of ivy growing abundantly across our high back wall. I could only watch him in admiration, scrambling upwards with his plimsolls gripping onto protruding bricks and small gaps of mortar and swinging across its top, avoiding ugly shards of glass stuck all along, prior to jumping down to join his girl waiting for him on that back road. In an instant I got wind of a sound of a car starting and driving off rapidly. Could Dimitri possibly avoid that journalistic hoard (and any local constabulary) who, without doubt, would now try finding and trapping him? Smiling inwardly and calling to mind his constant ability in past days as a communist spy to mask his trail, I was adamant my crony would win out.

I did not find out if Virginia's party saw light of day in such a turmoil that was to follow. That is of no import. In contrast, I must first talk about how that runaway duo got on in what was an amazing vanishing act by shaking off a vast cross country pursuit. (Much of this I was to find out about that coming night from national TV and my good doctor).

I am finding all this turmoil a knockout and so I must stop for a hiatus at this point. But I will inform you, first thing tomorrow, how my situation was to turn from critical to catastrophic.

XV

Our two runaways had just hit sixty driving south through occasional light local traffic, only to find out that, a short way back, a pair of howling squad cars was in hasty pursuit, alarms blaring and lights flashing. Pushing foot to floor, Barbara took a fast sharp right turn into a narrow winding country road to try to abscond.

In addition, flying low across a partly cloudy sky, a noisy pair of rotorcraft—a small Sikorsky and a British Army Air Corps WAH64—had now shown up to join in that hunt. Finally, any rustic calm which still might subsist in such a tranquil part of that pastoral county was totally lost as a long convoy of cars, full of paparazzi from all parts of our political panorama, was also madly chasing our absconding pair, aiming to outstrip both constabulary and rival hacks, in an audacious bid to scoop this astonishing gold bullion story.

For you to fully grasp just how vast was this accumulation of journalistic traffic, it is worth listing a full roll call of this frantic column of columnists. Right in front, as you might fancy, was that pack of Sun scandal hounds who had run away from Dimitri around midday, all now racing along in a bright crimson Toyota Corolla (with full sport pack, a giant airfoil on its boot lid, pallid walls on its Dunlops, bold racing strips along its doors and, stuck across its back window, a bold 'day-glow' sign proclaiming "I'm voting

Tory—RU?"). It had all and sundry within, shouting at a poor soul who was driving, to pull out a digit and hit a ton fast, or risk instant dismissal.

A short way back, in position 2, an uptight Daily Mail faction was trying to catch up in a Mini Clubman (with a tow bar on its back for a caravan), a car so full that its body was almost scraping along that tarmac. Within that small station wagon you could just distinguish, through its misty windows, a bunch of stalwart chaps, all sporting similar anoraks and all pounding away on laptops or phoning copy through to staff in London.

Following in a loud roar, a BMW sports saloon, its top right down, was full of Standard journalists (not that good at mornings and waking usually around midday) soporifically clutching pads and ballpoints or just holding on to hats in that brutal wind, and on its tail, a crowd from that good old Daily Mirror, was occupying a Vauxhall Corsa SRI, and, as if on a Sunday school outing, joining with gusto in a singsong of old pop hit ballads by UB40 playing loudly on its car radio—notably *"Kingston Town", "All I want to do"* and *"Until my dying day"*.

A gap of fifty yards, and you would also catch sight of a trio of law-abiding Guadrian (sic) staff in Barbour coats, driving slowly in a Volvo wagon—in fact submitting without fail to any signpost announcing a 30 or 40 or 50 mph limit as it was passing through a string of built up districts. Coming in last among this litany of motors dashing by, with locals watching in a trauma, was an unusual pair: a solitary individual from that Morning Star publication grimly frowning and driving a rusty old Lada, plus, finally in total contrast, a shiny Rolls, containing FT City staff, sporting sharply cut Higgins and Brown suits in luxury Italian fabric and looking forward to making a thorough listing and valuation of all that gold for a dramatic story to highlight in its forthcoming joint Saturday and Sunday publication. And as you might fancy, this FT car's colour was not gold—but pink!

Dusk was now falling rapidly. This obviously was a significant handicap for this wild hunt, particularly from up high, prompting both rotorcraft to switch on circulating spotlights for locating that runaway car, but without much luck.

Barbara was proving a skilful motorist, continuing to maintain a substantial gap in front of what was by now an outlandish swarm. (If you just thought for an instant of that famous childhood story, you could almost call our prima donna a "two colour flautist from a Brunswick town"—try working out that particular saying!) But this lady was now starting to worry, as a continual flashing coming from both patrol cars was slowly closing in. In addition a big "Halt" sign was indicating that this convoy was coming up to a major crossroads which would probably contain fairly thick traffic at this hour. It was crucial not to slow down. Barbara was also particularly anxious about traffic lights which might signify having to stop and in so doing, risking custody. Luckily on two occasions, that light was showing "go", so our runaways could carry on racing along.

But what was Dimitri up to as his plucky co-conspirator was racing onwards, with a flair you would normally only find among hoary participants in a tough car rally? In short our outwardly chauvinist Russian runaway was constantly phoning—almost oblivious of that frantic pursuit. In a world of his own, Dimitri, balancing his gold hoard firmly on his lap and cramming his smart pink Samsung pay-as-you-go communication apparatus tight against his cranium, was arguing, shouting, cursing, cajoling, laughing, bribing, indulging in blackmail or using various dubious tough-guy tactics with a pot-pourri of distant contacts. Mostly in Russian, now and again in our idiom, occasionally in schoolboy *français,* his phoning was continuing with hardly a gap for air. Finally with a howl of jubilation, this horticultural hoodlum flung down his buzz box and slid across to hug Barbara warmly, saying "*Milotchka*, my darling, our Houdini runaway plan is now all laid out. In orbit. It's lift off and go, go, go!"

This is how it was to work. Dimitri was always at pains to maintain top flight contacts with a now partly dormant communist UK spy matrix which had withstood Russia's political transformation, by mutating into an occult information and support unit for all sorts of dubious activity. His tortuous plan to vanish for good with his magic box was now drawn up in collaboration with that mafia, providing both could triumph in absconding from that madding crowd and would award that occult organisation with a bountiful cut. It was all laid out with Cold War rigour and imagination, involving a physical transformation of both runaways that would fool any constabulary, a nocturnal boat trip across to Normandy and many hours of driving across that Gallic nation to a hush-hush Swiss location.

By now, Dimitri was consulting his instructions and his road atlas, and starting to show slight signs of strain. "I won't go fully into this runaway plan of ours with you right now, Barbara—just trust your faithful suitor. But what's worrying is that our first port of call is still a fair way off, according to Mission Control. It simply calls for us to pinpoint a small isolation hospital lost in woodland half way twixt Paddock Wood and Cranbrook Common and obviously doing it incognito. But simply is hardly a fitting word, it could turn out a good hour's trip at this hour of today—and if that mob caught us up, that would imply curtains and prison bars for both of us."

Both sank into gloom as, with flashing lights closing in, it did now look as though captivity was not far off. But gradually a light bulb was starting to glow on top of Barbara's curly locks, as a prodigious solution for vanishing out of sight was slowly maturing in that lady's mind.

"It's my turn now for a visionary input, Dimi. Wait . . . just wait. That's it! Bingo! But could it work out? Yup, you can count on it. Why had I not thought of it until now?" Dimitri was curious about this outburst, but sat watching Barbara without saying a word.

This instant of inspiration had hit Barbara just as our duo was arriving in a quaint country town. And not any old town. In fact Barbara was born and brought up in and around this part of our world. Living as a child not fifty yards away from its Gothic Town Hall, passing through local infants' and junior schools, also a pupil graduating from its grammar school with flying colours to study Classics at Oxford (and gaining a First!), star of its church choir and county sports champion, Barbara did that small town proud. Now, coasting towards this locality's quaint old "Dog and Duck" inn, which was among our prima donna's habitual youthful haunts, a cunning and original gambit was about to play out.

This plan for shaking off that band in pursuit had struck Barbara using local know-how. It would imply taking a sharp turn off road and a solitary right turn across a rough cross country track, only known to occasional local inhabitants, starting from a small gap in a boundary wall which ran along that pub's grounds. Through that portal, you could wind for many furlongs across hilly grassland, roll along bumpy woodland paths and cross an occasional brook, finally coming out to join a narrow hilly road in a lost part of that county, which had only light traffic. This ran right down to our South Coast, passing not that far from Paddock Wood.

Turning sharply into that "Dog and Duck" car park and with Dimitri howling in horror at this surprising tactic, Barbara said firmly: "Don't ask what I'm doing Dimitri, just hold on to your hat and do as I say. This is probably our only opportunity for giving that gallant constabulary a slip. Our priority is first of all to swap cars. *Da, da,* my Russian plaything, I'm going to switch our transport.

"It's amazing, but it's a fact, my Grandpa John always parks his Honda saloon at this pub on any occasion that grand old man is away. And Grandpa is now on vacation in Thailand for a month. I can start using his motor this instant. I occasionally do. Grandpa will not mind. Look, as you can count on him constantly losing things, I always hold on to this for him—it's what starts his car's ignition. So, you and I can dump this jalopy now, jump into his and shoot across country incognito".

But could Barbara still find that crucial gap in that boundary wall to go motoring through? No doubt about it, it was still half way along. And crucially, no car was blocking it. Dimitri could only sit still and watch in fascination at his paramour's frantic activity. Barbara ran out smartly to unlock Grandpa's saloon, slid in, had its motor running in an instant, and was driving it smartly through that gap and onwards for thirty or forty yards. Straightaway Barbara was sprinting back, jumping in again with Dimitri, and driving that first car slowly up to that gap and positioning it firmly in front of it so as to block anybody following through in pursuit. Finally our champion was dragging a dumbstruck

Dimitri (and his box) physically out and pushing him into that runaway saloon.

Barbara was now racing off down into a rough grassy paddock, bumping wildly. Dimitri hanging on tightly to door grips and roof straps was in total shock now and had lost his calm "*Rady boga*, Barbara! What *is* all this about? Trying to kill us?"

"Stay cool. This is all familiar. And it's our vanishing act. I was always driving my old Morris Minor along this path long ago during our annual local off road rally. It's rough but worth trying."

As Barbara was saying this, a squad car was starting to turn in towards that pub and its occupants hastily climbing out. But that sight in a backwards mirror was to spur Barbara to switch off all car lights and—inconspicuous now—to count simply on a pallid moon for illumination in that gloaming, and also in this way, to avoid pinpointing by any rotorcraft still rumbling around on high.

A stalwart squad of constabulary, shouting loudly and waving guns at all and sundry had now run into Dog and Duck's public bar in a bid to trap our runaways—only to find that cosy snug full to bursting with mostly old locals indulging in its fortnightly pub quiz night. This group was plainly cross at such a dramatic disruption at a critical point in an all important match and was insisting on finishing that round prior to assisting in any way.

"Carry on you participants. Our visitors can wait a tick".

But a gruff patrolman was shouting: "I insist you stop now and you inform us if two audacious criminals ran in just now—and if so, say in what part of this pub our squad might find that pair hiding".

Without turning to look at him, that angry MC was ignoring this intrusion, stubbornly carrying on to finish that closing round—which was at a crucial point, with a count that stood at 42 to visitors and 44 to locals.

"Now it's our visitors' turn. This round is child's play. Which country sits south of Kyrgyzstan? Is it, Kazakhstan, Pakistan, Tajikistan or Afghanistan?"

"Look, Sir. I insist you stop this instant! Which way did that pair of daring crooks go?"

Nobody around that bar was stirring or saying a word. Winning that quiz championship was all important. Assisting a crowd of cops could wait. Local honour was at risk.

"Is it . . . Tajikistan?"

"Right, it is!" And a whoop of joy and wild clapping rang out.

"Back to our hosts now for this last conundrum. It's to do with railways and it's such a good'un to ask any of you lads and girls from this brainy inn! What famous British train did a USA tour just prior to World War Two?"

For a short instant you could latch onto a pin dropping . . . but a smiling old participant finally stood up.

"I think . . . it was a London, Midland and Scottish Railway Royal Scot class four-six-nought loco, known as Coronation Scot. It was on tour in Canada too!" A loud burst of clapping and raucous hurrahs was quickly drowning that MC's approval of his supposition. Dog and Duck had won. Rounds of local stout, whisky macs and a good many gin and tonics, in fact a bountiful supply of alcohol was starting circulating.

That band of cops had by now run through all floors and rooms of that inn and found nobody, apart from a barman and a barmaid indulging in flagrant passion up in an attic. On coming back down all glum among that happy carousal, a rapid invitation from partying locals to down a small dram prior to continuing that manhunt was forthcoming. A proposition that nobody in uniform could spurn.

Our duo was by now trailing across a rough grassy plot in total isolation, bumping up a stony cart track, splashing along a shallow brook and finally going up a slight hill into woodland through which ran a narrow path. Dimitri, still anxious, was moaning grumpily.

"Watch it, Barb, that log's in our way. You can't pick out anything in all this gloom. You will crash or run down into a ditch or a brook, obliging us to carry on by foot!"

But Barbara had a broad grin. "Just calm down, darling. Look up at that moon—it's coming out all bright and full now. And that inky sky is awash with stars. Stunning! Finding my way should not turn out too difficult now. Child's play, in fact. As for that madding crowd, you and I simply did our vanishing act and by now, all that constabulary caravan is bound to call it a day and abandon ship. That is . . . as long as our tank has that right amount for taking us as far as our final stop."

"What is it showing now?"

"Virtually dry, I'm afraid".

"Damn! It's just got to last that long. How far away do you think it is?"

"About thirty, I would say, Dimi. Just calm down. You and I must simply cross our digits. I fancy it would turn out much too risky for us to stop and fill up as soon as I'm back on a road. Can't show our mugs to anybody—you'd find radio and TV all carrying our story by now.

"How about a touch of soothing music? Arias from Puccini's Turandot or Black Magic Woman by Santana, do you think, or this disc of traditional jazz from my youth? Do you know, Dimi, I had a consummation of my first affair on this actual spot . . . in 'a shady nook by a babbling brook' as that old song says . . . all so romantic and so, so long ago".

"I don't wish to know that, thank you Barbara" was Dimitri's grumpy opinion.

This cross country trail was to last only half an hour. Soon our pair's car was coasting along a broad smooth path out of that woodland and winding down to join a country road. But a warning light was now shining on its dashboard. Filling up was crucial.

"How far away now?" Dimitri was holding his map right up to him as light was still poor.

"I would say—about two thousand yards. Cross your digits, you and I just cannot fail at this final curtain".

But that car did finally fail, coughing and jumping to a dramatic blackout, as that duo was coming up, again, to a country inn. Barbara took that opportunity to coast down to park among a throng of saloons and both took off sharply by foot.

"Wow! Almost at our goal. Just a short run for us along this footpath through this bit of woodland, if this map is right."

It was. You could not call that narrow trail, which both took, a path. No footway was obvious through all that thick scrubland and backwoods and in pitch black our pair was moving forward with difficulty. Running gasping through tall grass, tripping on brushwood and scrub, splashing in and out of muddy pools, wary of finishing up totally lost—until a vast dark block of buildings was looming in front. No obvious windows, no lights, crumbling masonry in parts with a small sign on its shabby main door saying "Warning! Isolation Hospital. No admission without a pass".

With a big grin and a knowing wink to Barbara, Dimitri rang at its door. From within, furious barking from a bloodthirsty pair of Alsatians was starting as a narrow horizontal hatch in that door slid smartly across and a scowling physiognomy was now filling it.

"What do you want?"

Dimitri put his lips right up against that window to proclaim softly that all-important password his contacts had said to him: "Tolstoy's cat has caught a fat rabbit"

A grunt from within, bolts roughly drawn back and that old door was thrust outwards as a blinding light from within lit up that absconding pair and that singular old box with its king's ransom within.

Back in that Dog and Duck pub, a gigantic party was by now in full swing in all its bars, with no room for anybody additional arriving. PCs and publicans, journalists and habitual patrons—all joining in a jolly bacchanalia, looking for consolation for losing track of our "criminals" so blatantly, subduing frustration at not landing a stunning scoop with such a mind blowing story or simply drinking away any chagrin at losing that national pub quiz cup. Blissful oblivion!

It is probably also worth noting that our PM got a call at 2 am from Barack Obama who was picking up this story from NBC, CBS and CNN, and was wanting to find out how much of a crisis this was turning into.

You could count on Sun journalists to sum it up succinctly that following morning. Across its top in bold black typography, our nation was told:

Gold rush—mighty crush

RUSSKY'S WILD SCOOT
WITH HISTORIC LOOT

A pair of Russian bandits was sort of found by a group of Sun journalists digging up a ton of lost gold loot and stuff in a South London park and skiving off with it all. But that dirty duo could not do a bunk from us Sun lot without us following, innit? And you know what? Our squad was on duty straightaway.

Soon a pair of CID patrol cars was kind of following us, in hot pursuit. It was a job for that band of boys in uniform (not us) to catch criminals and all that stuff, so our boys had to allow both cars to pass in front and that sort of thing, so as to collar that bunch of crooks.

But in only half an hour—what do you know?—our fabulous fuzz had lost track of that purloining pair who did a bunk—into thin air. Yawn!

So, look. Just go in for this Sun jackpot: A thousand pound bounty to anybody for information that assists in finding that pair or that loot, OK? Cool!"

XVI

So much for Dimitri's swift migration, how about my own flight away from all that woodland villainy? I did not stay to watch my collaborator's dramatic dash. It was crucial to withdraw instantly from all that was going on. I was not guilty of any conscious participation in that wrongdoing but who would trust my word for all that? I was bound to stand out as a joint conspirator.

In fact I had amazing luck in absconding with nobody noticing, thanks to my option not to run but to walk calmly and slowly as far as our way out. Racing off would only draw suspicion. And I had to do this out of sight of hoards of columnists and constabulary milling all around our parkland. Taking a solitary winding circuit through lost short cuts and minor paths, I was soon at our park's main portal, without having had contact with anybody from our staff as I did so. Now I had to find my way back to my flat, again inconspicuously.

Arriving at my bus stop, I found out to my distinct irritation that I had a fairly long wait again until my usual transport was to turn up. I thought it was judicious to stay out of sight and not to stand looking obvious by that busy road.

Unsurprisingly, my conclusion was that I ought simply to run across again into that charming church in front, hoping that, just as on my last visit, it was void of humanity.

I was lucky as on this occasion, it was without as much as an organist. So all I had to do was to sit calmly in that twilight sanctuary. In comparison with my first visit it was particularly dark, without any last rays of sunlight. "Just sit calmly" I was saying inwardly "And look at your watch"

But I was far from calm. It was hair-raising. I got to thinking I saw ghosts in that gloaming, so I was focussing constantly on my watch, willing it to hurry on. It was as if its hands had almost ground to a halt. My mind was hallucinating. Ghostly sounds, sharp sporadic cracks, noisy wings flapping high up in its roof, lights of cars flashing through its windows illuminating tombs and carvings, icy draughts blowing along its floor and a cold puff of air right across my brow. Was that a footfall up by that altar?

I sat numb, not daring to stir an inch until, finally, my watch was pointing out that my bus would shortly turn up. On my way out I was again to pass by that big box for church building fund donations standing by its door. I automatically put my hand into my slacks to look for cash as a thank you for this provisional sanctuary and got a shock by coming into touch with that handful of gold coins which was Dimitri's parting gift. It was obviously vital that I should discard that small stash which, if found in my custody, would simply imply my guilt in aiding Dimitri in his cardinal sin. But it would stand out as a worthy act on my part to slip that costly handful down through that slot in support of that grand church, in thanks for its shadowy asylum. I stood dropping my coins in singly, as I was trying hard to avoid any clanging sounds ringing throughout that holy location.

On board my bus at last, I was starting to calm down and act normally. It was not full and I was in luck, finding room to sit solo right up front downstairs—so avoiding any obligation for making small talk and any risk of anybody finding out who I was. A copy of that night's Standard was lying thrown away on that floor. Picking it up, I sat in shock, looking at its main story splashing across its front announcing "Gold bandits on run with historic hoard" with a big photo of Dimitri. It was comforting to find that it did not print my photo—luckily our parkland administration had not up to this point got round to taking my snapshot for its display. I was wanting to pick up all I could about that manhunt, and to find out if I was among any black list. But I was also happy simply to hold that journal out fully, just an inch or two from my brow as if I was myopic, hiding my physiognomy from all on board!

I was virtually dozing off as my bus was arriving at my local stop and I got up and off as calmly and inconspicuously as I could. My plan on arriving back at my flat was to contact Doctor Smith (who, by now, was bound to know all about Dimitri's monstrous misappropriation) and solicit his aid in coping with this quandary I was in. Though not guilty, it was obvious that I could not carry on working for now in that parkland. I had to vanish until all was calm again.

But on turning finally into my road, I had to stop short as I saw, not fifty yards in front, that my normally tranquil locality was all lit up with tall floodlights, full of prying crowds and frantic activity—constabulary cars, TV vans with various sorts of dish on top and, worst of all, a myriad of journalists, phoning, noting things down or simply milling around. It was plain that I was a fatal attraction and about to fall into a trap.

I did a smart about turn to start slowly ambling away. Coming to a busy shopping mall and walking right across its car park until I was lost among its rubbish bins, I put a call through to my saviour. Luckily Doctor Smith was in and *au fait* with my quandary.

"Could you quickly find a taxi around you? . . . Good. Ask him to go to Windsor railway station and to drop you in front. I'll start driving to it now in a Subaru 4x4 with black windows and link up with you at its car park's north boundary. It's all dark in that particular spot. As soon as I stop, you just climb into my boot".

It all had a sound of a corny cold war spy story, but it was my only option and it was to work out brilliantly. Within an hour and a half, I was lying chin on thighs in a tight spot but in good hands, and making a trustworthy withdrawal from a dramatic situation.

What a day! But in finalising this narration for my diary, I must add a postscript about what was to occur following my flight from that church. Its vicar—God grant him aid—did his daily round at nightfall to lock up his church, including taking out all donations for that day. His bishop got a rapturous call. "My Lord, it's nothing short of miraculous. Good tidings of joy to all mankind. In our box I usually find a paltry handful of small coins, tiddlywinks and buttons—or occasionally a 50p but today . . . today it's all gold. A good handful of it. A prodigious transformation—thanks to our Almighty."

Within half an hour, local radio and TV had this story, portraying it as a prodigious act of "turning H2O into Grand Cru Burgundy" and giving it top priority. Finally, thousands of locals crowding around that church took part in an all night vigil of worship and thanksgiving.

XVII

A word now in passing as to how I can supply all this information about Dimitri's triumph in vanishing into thin air with his booty (and his consort), whilst a frantic throng of British and Gallic constabulary in hot pursuit could only draw a blank.

During that following fortnight, I had a chain of long mails from my old horticultural companion turn up surprisingly on my laptop, with a blow by blow account of how both had found that wily way to abscond. I also got a follow up call from him announcing his arrival with his darling at a final distant sanctuary and saying a last poignant "so long, it was good to know you" and "*oudatcha!*"

But may I just start taking you back to that outwardly rundown isolation hospital building and Dimitri's cryptic password to gain admission. Our two runaways ran hastily through that dirty old door, passing a duo of tough looking guards (both having a pair of pistols handy) into a brilliantly lit building, which had a look of a futuristic film studio. It was all glass partitions, automatic sliding doors and shiny floors, digital indicator boards along long corridors to various wards, young blond staff in stylish outfits, warm air-conditioning, and background music by Borodin playing softly, occasionally giving way to vocal information in both Russian and our own idiom.

Whilst Barbara sat anxiously in a waiting hall, Dimitri clutching tightly his box of gold was shown into a dark soundproof room, to sit for an hour with two tall grim looking apparatchiks in a stormy discussion of final conditions for dividing his hoard. Finally with smiling and vigorous backslapping all round, Dimitri was to hand his compatriots two fifths of his booty. So now, that work on his physical transformation could truly start.

Within two jolts of a lamb's tail, you could find Dimitri and Barbara with scant clothing lying flat out on top of individual surgical platforms in a floodlit room. A man in doctor's garb was busy working painstakingly, changing totally both runaways' looks. This individual was probably Britain's paramount prodigy in facial and bodily disguising, and had had a brilliant history of working for film and TV studios on major stars (particularly in horror films). Through his skilful handiwork in applying various masking products, Dimitri's skin was slowly turning into a mass of burns, bruising, frightful scabs and flaky crusty lumps—a ghastly sight. In fact it was such a convincing transformation that any consultant, who was an authority on critical skin complaints, might put forward a diagnosis of pityriasis chronica or von Zumbusch psoriasis. What was most important was that looking at him as hard as you could, you would not in a month of Sundays say this was Dimitri.

Changing Barbara's look was not such a difficult task. It was simply about making this lady look a young man with short hair and a stubbly chin. Barbara also had to put on military clothing to pass off as an army motorist.

With such dissimulations intact, both now took custody of a long khaki hospital wagon (with a blood colour cross on its doors and roof). Barbara sat up front driving whilst

Dimitri lay horizontal in its back (with his box snugly out of sight). And so, that final link in this chain of withdrawal from our world was about to start.

It was at first a calm and smoothly running trip—although Barbara had many a worry with squad cars racing by, though not stopping. Both got quickly into a calm driving rhythm—not too fast and not too slow.

First port of call was Dymchurch. A fast launch was waiting in a solitary spot, driving on board took just an instant with no control from its customs' post which was vacant all that night (vital information from our Russian contacts—so showing passports was not an obligation). A calm crossing to Wissant took just two hours. Finally, landing in Normandy was in no way arduous and that runaway wagon was soon cruising happily along fairly vacant motorways.

In fact it was mostly a humdrum trip, passing placidly from Calais through Arras, Laon, Châlons, Toul and Colmar, halting, following four hours' driving, for a short pit stop in a shady spot by a food hall for a sandwich, a soft drink and a short but obligatory half hour nap. All going to plan.

Until, that is, about half an hour from that Swiss boundary. Traffic was gradually grinding to a halt on account of a CRS road block. An assiduous patrol was making occasional cars and trucks pull in to go through inquiry and scrutiny. It had put this manhunt in hand following a brutal burglary in Rouffach, at which a civic dignitary was shot and a haul of cash lost.

During this slow crawl, Barbara was practising talking in a low pitch, as a man would, and trying to think of any basic Gallic vocabulary which had hung around from schooldays. How should you start translating that Dimitri had draconian burns all across his body and was on his way to a Swiss clinic to submit to critical nursing to bring his skin back to normal? Barbara was cross for not having thought of bringing a bi-lingual dictionary for this sort of occasion.

On arriving at that road block, a tough looking official hastily put out an arm and was indicating to Barbara to pull in and alight for quizzing. A curious discussion was soon to occur in a mix of idioms—both participants having a worthy try at bi-lingual communication.

"To what town do you go?"

"*Nous allons à un hôpital à Zurich*"

"Nationality?"

"*Anglais*—oh, I should say British"

"But your car has diplomatic markings. Show us your passport."

Barbara's muscular organ for pumping blood was now racing. This could truly put a cat among a crowd of small stout birds that coo constantly, thousands of which you can find in London's tourist spots. Total anonymity was crucial for both to vanish for good.

"*Un instant!* I am going to look for it dans *l'auto*"

"*D'accord.* But as you do it, I must ask to look in back of wagon".

Barbara, by now most anxious was shouting at him.

"*Non, s'il vous plaît, il y a un ami mourant.* Critically ill"

But a companion of his in uniform was by now lifting up that wagon's back door. Taking a quick look in, a loud gasp rang out from that poor soul, who was backing away in shock at that gory sight of Dimitri's skin. As our Russian, conscious of all that was said during this inquisition, was now starting to groan loudly as if in stabbing pain, this functionary softly shut that door back down again, shouting a flood of anxious words to his boss. Straightaway this official put on a distraught air, standing back to start waving Barbara onwards with frantic hand signals.

In fact on driving off from that tricky control point, Barbara found that a CRS car was now right in front with its roof lights flashing, so as to unblock any slowly moving traffic in our way. It was to accompany our pair rapidly as far as that critical Swiss crossing point, just a short run from a final sanctuary.

"Cool!" was Barbara's summary to Dimitri of that amazing affair, as that pair at last saw a road sign indicating that Zürich was but thirty km to go.

"Hot stuff", said our invalid, chuckling now. "Wait till I start writing my book about all this".

XVIII

"How can I possibly thank you, Doctor Smith, for all your lavish pains and for taking such risks to spirit my poor old body away from that witch hunt?"

I was sitting in his warm study with my hands around a giant mug of hot cocoa, savouring a tasty round of mushrooms on toast and starting to calm down from my string of traumas.

"You should not carry on saying that, Paul. As your consultant, it was my duty to rally round to bail you out from your drastic quandary. It was also a bit of fun to run rings around Old Bill. In fact it all has had a flavour of a Bond spy story, don't you think?"

"But no hold ups. Or voluptuous girls, sadly!" I said, smiling.

Doctor Smith was now looking my way with a slightly disapproving air.

"I must say, though, that it was a bit hasty of you to offload your bounty in that church, as you said you had, probably with prints of your digits or your DNA on that handful of coins you put in that box. And no doubt your photo will show up shortly in print and on TV as soon as your flat is put through full scrutiny and your snap album is found. You must go to ground".

I had nothing to add. My physician was right. I had blown it and I was nodding.

"So what will you do about that cat of yours?"

"Just now I put a call through to an old chum with a flat two doors away along my road who is totally trustworthy and who is always happy to mind my companion for as long as I wish".

"Good. I ask this as it's obvious you must go far away incognito until all this dust is horizontal. Paul, I want to put a proposition to you. But prior to doing so, I am right in thinking, am I not, that you still cannot talk using any words containing that barbarian?"

"I still can't, I'm afraid."

"I thought so. But I know that your capacity for talking almost normally has grown strikingly. It's not just satisfactory now, but truly skilful. In fact, you might say, with no obligation on your part to go back to using a full ABC."

"That's probably right".

"You will no doubt call to mind from our symposium at Clapham Junction that our Oulipo organisation in Paris has many important tasks on its books, including a multi-lingual clinic for studying original ways of improving communication among its participants. In fact, just this month, our plan is to start a school for instructing that local Gallic Oulipolitburo in talking in our British idiom without using that antagonist. And that's a thing you now do admirably. So, how about you taking on that job and running that class? You cannot carry on working in your parkland, can you? And as you must put down roots far away for now, Paris is a good solution. In addition, Oulipo would pay you royally for your input—four thousand in local cash a month. And it would maintain a wary watch on you as you go around. How do you fancy that proposition?"

I was aghast. It was such an intriguing opportunity and such a smart way to jump ship. "Wow! That sounds an amazing solution. What can I say but *d'accord?*" But how can I land up in Paris incognito?"

Doctor Smith was smiling at my angst: "I was in fact planning to go across soon to visit my contacts and discuss plans for our World Symposium in Burkina Faso this Autumn. My diary is fairly blank this coming fortnight and my assistant can fill in for any minor consultations on our books. So, if it suits you, both of us could go tomorrow morning."

"Good Lord! So soon. Many thanks—but with all our country on a lookout, what would I do about passport control?"

Doc—as I was starting to call him—was smiling impishly: "Did you mind too much riding along in my car boot just now?"

I was grinning too. "It was tight. But an apt solution. Now I'm following you"

"Through customs in this way—and it always works. So I could magic you onto a train via—to put it in our colourful way of talking—that long cavity dug all that way across to Normandy".

"Brilliant. I'm with you!"

Doc shook my hand warmly, adding: "And finally, just to inform you, I am hanging on to all your almost daily accounts which I trust you will go on writing and submitting. As soon as your final word is said, I am proposing that you and I publish it all as a book—for ordinary humans to savour. It will turn out worth it, as it's an astounding story. No doubt about it!"

XIX

How comforting it is to find I am back in Paris again. Calm and nonchalant in knowing that I am far away from all that turmoil raging in London, I am now savouring all this stimulating city's attractions on what is such a radiant sunny day. I had my initial baptism into this happy hunting ground in my youth a good many moons ago, during a fortnight's holiday with my school's sixth form class, following which Paris has always sat on top spot of my "away from it all" list.

My runaway trip with Doc ran finally without a hitch. So I shall avoid giving you a blow-by-blow account of our various minor ups and downs. His plan for my hiding in his car boot was to work out admirably. I will admit that I did occasionally twitch with misgivings, particularly as I lay curling up in a tight ball, almost dying with cramp, as our car was arriving at a final control point prior to driving on board a train. A customs man, holding on to a snarling sniffing dog, was shouting at us. But far from commanding us to stop and—God forbid—lift up our boot lid, this official was abruptly signalling us onwards, straight onto our train bound for Calais.

Add on an hour or so, and our car was stationary in a motorway lay-by just south of that town, with our windows down to allow us to savour a good many lungfuls of cool crisp air. I was now sitting up in front with my jubilant companion, drinking a cold can of *Badoit*, wiping my brow and soothing my numb limbs.

I must say that it was not until our car was running into that busy circular highway around Paris that I was gradually unwinding and my angst did not vanish totally until Doctor Smith was drawing up in front of a classic portico on top of which I saw, cut in bold gold capitals, that comforting inscription—OULIPO.

From my first introduction, I had bountiful input from our local Oulipians. Thanks to such convivial companions, I quickly found a compact but practical fifth floor studio flat to inhabit for six months, just north of Vavin subway station. (If I may just on this occasion opt for a US word for this form of transport!). My accommodation is in a handy district of this city. Of a morning I stroll not thirty yards from our front door to two important shops that satisfy my basic daily wants. First, a traditional loaf baking *magasin*, crucial to providing a long thin warm crusty stick to start my day (with lashings of apricot jam). And adjoining this paragon stands a classic Parisian bistro to which I go to savour my mid-morning cappuccino.

What I find particularly alluring about this pair of habitual ports of call is that multiplicity of ambrosial aromas which waft outwards, a fatal attraction to anybody walking by. For a drink or a snack, I invariably opt for this sort of bar with its own distinct spirit, its squad of *garçons* always in a hurry, noting down and bringing back what you ask for, or pouring out with a flourish an abundant array of drinks. It's an oasis that has an intrinsic part to play in this town.

Not having paid a visit to this "City of Light" for far too long, I am sad to find in so many districts nowadays a mushrooming of boring uniform global imports such as Barsucks, Costalot and Macdon't, all lacking any charisma or individuality as to its products or its layout and all slowly driving typical local bistros into bankruptcy.

Anyway, by mid-morning today I was found sitting comfortably in what is now my usual spot by a window in my customary bistro for watching Parisians ambling by, improving my skills in this local way of communicating by dipping into a copy of Paris Match and that morning's Figaro and also consulting my bilingual Collins dictionary. This was my last day of furlough prior to launching my Oulipo class and so it was crucial that I also rack my brains about how to plan my tutorials within my vocal limitations.

Obviously, having to stand up and talk, clarify or justify my input in my own idiom, ought not to occasion any major worry. My good Doctor is to thank for that. But I am anticipating that topics will sporadically occur with my pupils which I can only sort out by switching into local vocabulary (minus you know what), and such a probability is starting to look particularly scary. Up to this point, by counting on my schoolboy vocabulary, I had not had any particular difficulty in finding and using a sporadic "virtuous" local word. But my ability to launch into any continuous profound discussion with my class in its own lingo was starting to look truly doubtful.

At first I thought it fun to work my way word by word through that pair of local journals, looking for vocabulary I could say. But my antagonist was turning up with alarming constancy in all I was scrutinising. Doctor Smith had said that this "black animal"—as locals might call it—was found in cataclysmic proportions in this lingua franca. Its British variant was mild in comparison. And so I quickly found out. In drawing up my OK Paris word list, I had to discard all but a tiny minority of nouns, pronouns and so on as taboo.

My initial quixotic goal was to amass a hoard of up to a thousand Oulipo words by nightfall—a ludicrous ambition! In fact by midday and my third cup of invigorating potion, my catch was looking sorrowful, although it did contain a short list of basic units of communication, as follows: *Oui* and *non, bonjour* and *bonsoir, s'il vous plaît, pardon*, *d'accord* and *bravo, voici* and *voilà, bon* and *mauvais, j'ai faim* and *j'ai soif, à propos, ça va, du bon vin, ça fait mal, à la maison . . . ,*

But I quickly ground to a halt. I could not at first call to mind a local construal of "thank you" or "how much?" My solution to that duo was *parfait!* and *dis-moi son prix.* Both of which struck my mind as skilful thinking. From shops and stalls, I could ask about availability of any product by saying that handy formula *y a-t-il?* As for quantity, I could only buy *un kilo* or *trois* or *cinq* and so on.

Also, although I cannot say "I" in this land, I could always fall back on *moi*—and so for translating "I want" I could just say *pour moi.* But so much vocabulary just did not find its way into my mouth. I was thinking back to that flamboyant display of synonyms at Clapham Junction.

What if I wish to say any form of a word portraying an action or condition following pronouns such as *vous, il or ils?* I found no magic potion. I would just go back to communicating with hand signals as if I was dumb. No, for a quantum jump forward in all this confusion, I would simply dip again into *La Disparition*—that original and amazing Oulipopular classic book, which was a parting gift from Doc, and try to find in its most original and humorous narration a host of colourful solutions to my critical word block.

I am straying now and should go back to composing this daily dispatch. Paris is a city for admiring on foot and, as it was warm, my plan today was to criss-cross its midst, slowly taking in again all its sumptuous sights. By 2 pm I was out and about and basking in all its glory. But it was difficult to throw off that gloomy cloud of worry about my diction lurking in my mind. That diabolical sign was a fixation. I could not avoid it. In particular, as I was passing by that myriad of famous sights, I was not up to actually naming any out loud. Just think. If I was guiding visitors around this city's sights, how could I triumph?

A possibility was, I thought, to try baptising such tourist attractions with synonyms in my own vocabulary? I found that I could, just about, partly in straight translation and partly by using long paraphrasing. So all aboard for my Oulipopular tour of Paris:

"From in front of "Our Lady", that magical giant sanctuary of Christian worship rising up grandly from "City Island", I start ambling along that famous "Right Bank", continuing through that historic mass of royal palatial buildings along its rim, with its world famous accumulation of works of art. I stop and gasp at its vast glass pyramid and imposing formal courtyards. Managing at last to run (suicidally!) across that gigantic "Concord" crossroads, avoiding all that non-stop racing traffic, I am found finally striding up that grand broad road towards Paris' most famous symbol, which I am bound to call its "Triumphal Arch".

By four o'clock I was sitting glumly in a small bistro half way up that world famous highway, watching, through its tall glass doors, a constant flow of tourists ambling along in a happy go lucky fashion. I still could not rid my mind of that "ominous tiny round animal with a big grin". Or if I was looking at writing in capitals, I could call it that "horizontal toasting fork". I saw it all around—on road and shop signs, on city road plans, or on publicity displays across any bus that was passing by. If I had to look at a city transport map, it was plain that virtually all Paris stations contain my antagonist. I was simply hallucinating at any sight of that tantalising ghost continually laughing at my discomfort. I would just stay dumb from now on.

Back that night in my cosy sanctuary, following a glass or two (or four!) of cool Chablis to calm that gravity in my brain, I sat down to watch a thrilling football match on TV in which Poland won against Italy, four goals to two. It was such a tonic to iron out my worn out mind. What I did was turn down its frantic sound and just watch, so that it was all about playing and nothing about saying. By midnight I was back to normal and sitting calmly working out my tutorial formats. I was in fact starting to look forward to it all, in particular as it was obvious that my pupils with a similar liability could in fact act as my coach in improving my local vocabulary. *Cocorico!*

XX

I got to Oulipo HQ promptly for my first day's class, almost an hour in fact prior to any of my pupils. My goal in so doing was to monitor thoroughly a spacious fourth floor auditorium in which I was to carry out my tuition—looking at its layout, its audio visual apparatus, lighting, flip chart pads and writing aids. I also had to find out if it had good air conditioning—I do occasionally sustain a touch of claustrophobia in such locations.

As for my tutorials, I had drawn up a basic format and a long list of topics to follow in my first class or two, an input which I could quickly modify and build on as I was going along, should I confront any snags or shortcomings in my approach. This coaching job was still an unknown world in which I had to amplify my skills and gain aplomb.

So it was with growing misgivings that I rang a big brass button on Oulipo's palatial door on that initial occasion. It was quickly ajar, and I was shown in by a tall lordly looking African, whom I initially simply thought of as a doorman. But I rapidly got to know him as administrator in control of all of Oulipo's scholastic activity—a kindly practical man with a fascinating background. Ahmadou was from Ivory Coast, born in Yamoussoukro and brought up in Abidjan, talking in Victor Hugo's idiom from childhood, with *dioula* (a variant of *bambara*) as his main local patois. Study in a Catholic high school in Mons and sojourns in world famous institutions such as Harvard and Oxford had brought him imposing qualifications.

But Ahmadou was born with our common flaw—an inability for coping with that fifth sign. That said, communication in writing was no handicap for him and winning a major scholarship to study in Paris was his bid to find a solution to his faulty articulation.

Making our way up to my classroom, our approach to chitchat was thus basic, bi-lingual, but instantly full of good humour. Ahmadou would say an odd word in his old colonial diction (or occasionally in my own vocabulary or with a touch of *franglais*) using vigorous hand signals and I would try hard to talk back sagaciously in my national idiom, throwing in a word or two of local Parisian patois.

Arranging that auditorium to my satisfaction was quick to accomplish. As I was now simply waiting for my pupils to turn up, I was practising my tuition, with my Ivorian companion watching through a small oblong window up high in his control cabin, catching what I was saying, judging my didactic skills, grinning and giving a kindly thumbs up (or occasional thumbs down) sign during my solo dry run.

So I was in good spirits as my class was slowly arriving. It was surprising to find that I had almost thirty scholars in total, all plainly anxious to start improving any primary ability in using my way of talking. At first our mutual contact was a touch formal with much shaking of hands and habitual salutations passing among us in this or that idiom. To a cautious *bonjour, j'ai pour nom . . . . François,* I said a warm "good morning" or "hi! I'm Paul" or "glad to know you. I trust you'll find our class fruitful".

Introductions out of our way, with my stomach churning, I got busy with my first topic—basic colloquial vocabulary—by slowly voicing a list of straightforward groups of words for all to chant back in parrot fashion. To "crack any glacial H2O" with my group, I thought I would simply launch into my tuition with a short fatuous saying which, according to Ahmadou, was traditionally taught to young Parisian schoolboys and girls in a first contact with my idiom: "Will you all kindly say: My tailor is rich"

An occasional spot of giggling ran around as my class was intoning this absurd proposition. But most of my pupils visibly did not find such an introductory gambit particularly amusing. It was obvious that my initial contact was proving a humiliating *faux pas*. It was too soon for joking.

So I had to start again. In contrast, I would now try to build up a good rapport with my group by outlining straightforwardly how I was going to approach my instruction, both in this first contact and onward throughout forthcoming workshops. Luckily this frank clarification hit a right button. By its conclusion, my pupils had caught my mood and from that instant I found it plain sailing to focus on my list of topics for all to join in and commit to mind.

My first list of sayings was to do with going shopping.

"How much will it cost?" "Only four pounds fifty." "That's a bargain".

All had a try at parroting this Q and A, but with such poor diction that I had to ask my group to try saying it all again. It was still mumbo jumbo:

"Aoo moosh vill it cost? Onlii foorr poondz fiifti. Zatz a bargayn"

It was a worthy shot but still way off track. Anyhow, accuracy in pronunciation was, I thought, not a crucial factor to instil in my scholars initially. It was basic communication that was important—to commit to mind a copious stock of valid groups of "good" words. How to actually say such words with accuracy could wait. So I took my flock back to "visiting Harrods":

"On what floor will I find shirts and coats?"

"That's too much. I am looking for a bargain"

"Do you stock anything similar in a dark colour, such as black or brown?"

"Can I pay you with a plastic card?"

"I will pick it up tomorrow morning. Is that all right?"

I quit this topic of buying goods by moving on to a broad array of handy phrasing in a multiplicity of situations, with my class by now joining in to mimic my diction with practically no inhibition.

"A pint of draught, a malt whisky and a small glass of Chablis, if you don't mind"

"But your honour, I was only doing thirty along this road"

"I'm lost. Can you point out my position now on this map? Thank you".

"What do you do all day at work in front of your PC?"

"No smoking in this bar I'm afraid, sir. You must go outdoors. Sorry!"

Having built up a good rhythm, I was by now tackling a topic that all of us Britons pass our days constantly talking about—actual or forthcoming climatic conditions. Normal folk would obviously sum it all up with a short common noun (starting with a "w") which you could sing about as "stormy" but which nobody among us could possibly say out loud. Still, all of us could chat about it, in truth for hours, and launch into a thorough discussion of microscopic variations of what our Good Lord up in his sky could hold out for us on a daily basis.

"What a glorious warm sunny day—Not a cloud in sight"

"Strong north winds will blow, I am told, and snow will fall by tonight"

"You ought to bring a brolly. It looks as if it might rain. Don't you think so?"

"Wrap up warmly if you go out this frosty morning and don't slip on that icy road, will you?"

"It was said on TV last night that it could turn cold and foggy"

As by now my class had shown a fairly good grasp of my idiom, I thought I would pass on to a witticism which I had found through a bit of googling on my PC:

"Do you know that funny story about an Anglo-Saxon, an Irishman and a Scotsman?" No, my class did not, but was curious to fall for it.

"An Anglo Saxon, an Irishman and a Scotsman sit in a pub. This trio all hold a pint of stout, individually watching a fly land in all that thick froth on top of his glassful. Our British man in horror can only pour his drink away. Our Scotsman dips his thumb in his drink, flicks out that fly and sups his stout with gusto. But our Irishman picks up his fly, holds it by its wings on top of his glass and shouts at it: "Spit it out! Spit it out!""

Much chuckling and a round of clapping was grand acclaim for this frail opus.

Thus, although it had a slow start, my first class was a hit. From that point on, drawing up my scholastic syllabus was plain sailing. I had won sympathy and good will from my pupils. Follow-up tutorials (our plan was to run four such sittings twixt Monday and Friday, lasting an hour and a half) had a pot-pourri of formats—partaking in a vocabulary quiz, working in duos to talk about a particular activity such as "what I did last Sunday" or "what I plan to do tomorrow", "my most amusing *faux pas*" or "my most unusual holiday". Or to obtain input about family history—"a dish or two from my grandma's cookbook" or "what my granddad did in World War Two". With such voluntary participation, I got quickly into a gratifying and not too arduous rhythm and found that drawing up class formats was not at all difficult. Many of my pupils put forward proposals. In fact many did so by writing scripts for acting out amusing situations, saving any labour on my part.

In addition, my work was soon attracting plaudits from Oulipo top brass. I also had abundant congratulations from Doctor Smith who, told of my triumph, shot across a long congratulatory mail to my in-box, pointing out that my original approach to tuition was attracting substantial curiosity among important top brass in various official administrations in Paris.

I was always thankful to Ahmadou who was a constant aid in my activity. Insuring that I got fitting support from his board in all I did, this companion was happy passing hours staring through his small window at my antics, whilst guiding my activity by various signs of his big black thumb. In turn I was using various hand signals back to him, to solicit *"lights on full", "lights down"* or *"play that DVD again"* and so on.

Tout à fait parfait! That is—until about a fortnight into my curriculum. Finalising a short dictation at about 4pm, I was to turn, without any warning, faint and slightly giddy. So I thought it was crucial to signal an *"air con high"* instruction to my collaborator. But on glancing up towards that small window, I had a mighty shock. An unusual physiognomy was filling that oblong in contrast to my African champion. It was a Caucasian man who had a most familiar look, which I thought I had caught sight of in many situations in Paris. Was it on TV? In journalism? Just who was this individual I was looking at? In an instant that mythical man was to vanish and Ahmadou's dusky grin was back.

I had quickly drawn my class to a conclusion and as soon as I had said: "Mind how you go" to my last pupil, I was rushing up into our control box to ask Ahmadou who it was who was spying transitorily on my tuition. Ahmadou was fairly taciturn, not grinning as was his wont.

"I don't know who that individual was—from a Ministry or an official scholastic organisation, I should think. I am not always told about our visitors. Our boss is constantly asking without any warning if I might allow this or that functionary or cultural authority to sit in for a short stint to monitor just how a typical syllabus of ours is run."

"But Ahmadou, I am dumbstruck. I cannot think this was just any old sort of visitor. That man I saw staring just now at my antics through your window is famous. I know him. It sounds stupid to say it, but I would say without a shadow of a doubt that it was that man who is running this country".

My companion did not flinch, maintaining a laid back look. "Calm down, Paul, you must try not to work so hard", was his consolatory diagnosis. But it did not halt my confusion.

"You might think it was just a hallucination. Or that I drank too much Gigondas at lunch. And I am not on drugs. But you know that postal stamp you can buy today with its imposing portrait of Nicolas Sarkozy at his coronation—that's whom I saw as plainly as anything on show through that oblong skylight. A spitting copy".

Ahmadou took on a painful air and put his hand on my arm: "*Voyons, mon ami*. What you maintain is just ludicrous. Do you think for an instant that our national capo has any gap in his busy diary to run across town and spy craftily on a small class of loquacious misfits? I think, Paul that you should opt for a day or two off."

In confusion, I was nodding in accord with my Ivoirian collaborator.

"As you will. I will not go on about it. It was not royalty, if you say so. I'll start taking things slowly this Saturday and Sunday. But frankly, you could not fail to spot a distinct similarity, now could you?"

Ahmadou, closing down his audio visual unit, shot a knowing look my way, put his digit to his lips, adding a long conspiratorial wink.

XXI

A fortnight on from my last tidings, I must inform you that my situation has again had an astounding transformation. My Oulipo class is now run by Ahmadou (using my curriculum admirably, I am told) and I am not now a daily visitor to its HQ. Why? In fact I had a surprising call two days ago from a functionary in a Ministry in this capital with an invitation (a stipulation in fact) to switch from that cosy informal syllabus I was running with my young group and to start conducting hush-hush individual tutorials with a handful of high ranking national administrators.

It was at first a shock to find out that among top Ministry staff in Paris a surprising proportion should show symptoms of my sort of dysphasia. But this is Paris and I just had to call to mind that it was, in point of fact, a Gallic author who was first, of anybody in our world, to concoct and publish a pot-pourri of oulipopular writings. So it was logical that this curious difficulty with articulation might occur significantly throughout this country, right up into its ruling class!

Just try imagining my situation now: first thing of a working day, a shiny spacious official black car, with dark windows and a burly Tunisian in uniform driving, draws up in front of my block of flats and as soon as I am on board, whisks off to an imposing Ministry building on Quai d'Orsay.

Driving through its broad classical portico, passing an abundant accumulation of historical busts and carvings, my transport stops in a spacious courtyard in front of a spiral stairway. A major-domo, saluting, pulls my door towards him and I climb out and up, to pass through a circular portal. I am now in a vast hall with high Corinthian columns and capitals and bright colourful floors portraying in mosaic, various national military triumphs. Up in a lift to its fourth floor and I now find I am walking along a classical corridor with walls hung with tall mirrors in gilt mouldings and with striking oil paintings of many a famous king or politician or valiant national dignitary. Half way down and to my right I finally stop in front of a plain brown door sporting a brass sign indicating "four-six-six". My classroom—or I should call it my study. I occupy it solo.

In this bright and light sanctuary, with high windows facing south and sunlight pouring in, I find a spacious and stylish mahogany work station, a laptop, various rows of books, in particular dictionary upon dictionary for consulting if I am doing translations, a blackboard with chalks, a mini-bar (that's right, I am lucky) with a contraption for making hot drinks, and also a door through to a small cloakroom. Hung on two of my walls I can look in admiration at a stunning group of original lithographs by famous artists such as Pablo Picasso, Joan Miró and Raoul Dufy.

I sit in a soft high back armchair in total luxury, facing a third wall—an unusual sort of partition of cloudy glass, so dark in fact as to obstruct any vision through to any occupant sitting and working in that contiguous accommodation. In my instructions I was told that my various "pupils" would occupy—individually and incognito—that adjoining room, with an ability to watch my own input in total clarity as both of us work in unison. It was all at first slightly off-putting, but by now I can carry off my function with aplomb.

In addition, from my first day, a strict format was laid down as to how I was to run my tutorials. I taught six "anonymous" pupils—all in fact functioning with cryptic IDs, such as *Strasbourg vingt-six* or *Toulon noir* or *Lyon sous-marin*. An individual class was to last a maximum of an hour, mostly in a discussion of a topic particularly significant to a pupil's individual portfolio in this organisation. Within days, formality which was a trait in our initial contacts was making way for a cordial complicity—I was using that *"tu"* form—and joking was paramount.

On account of a wish by this Ministry for total privacy surrounding my function, I could not join staff in any dining room, but a sumptuous lunch was brought to my room at half past noon, always including a glass or two of its outstanding *vin du mois* (this month a *Mouton Rothschild Pauillac*).

If any gaps did occur in my "transmural" instruction rota, particularly following lunch, I took on various ancillary tasks, such as composing official orations for any of my "invalids" to affirm on a visit to UN HQ in Manhattan, laying out this country's position on an array of topics. I soon found it all child's play to do scrupulously unambiguous translations using convincing oulipolitical Anglo-Saxon jargon.

Or I might also find I was participating in planning for an official visit to Paris by a diplomatic mission from abroad to discuss a particular sticking point on policy. Two days ago, this Ministry had a visit from USA's Food and Drug Administration on soaring global consumption of salt, sugar and fat and how all this could harm our world population's constitution. It was a fascinating window on our humanity.

Finally, in my solitary lair, I occasionally had to adjust a final wording of an official policy proclamation, by fishing out "no go" words which nobody among my "pupils" could say in public and by putting in straightforward analogous vocabulary. This is an illustration of my diplomatic thumbs down to a proposal, originally containing many an ambush:

"Your point is obviously important and will obtain full scrutiny from us all, obliging our ambassador to study its implications thoroughly. Our policy in such conditions is to consult any party with rights and claims in this affair. My country is thus not in favour of that particular wording and would favour a diplomatic and truly global accommodation".

Ah! Diplomacy is, indubitably, a word happily void of that fatal sign, don't you think?

XXII

Following a long run of mild sunny days, this morning was chilly and dismally damp. It was not just raining. Paris was sustaining a mighty downpour. So I thought that to avoid a soaking I would stay by a window in my flat looking down, until I could spot my car to work drawing up at my door. It was not as punctual as usual and as soon as I saw what I thought was my transport stopping, I ran downstairs (our lift was faulty) and automatically got straight in.

But I had a monstrous shock in passing through its back doorway. This was not my customary lift. Nor was it my usual taciturn companion in front who was driving. It was a suspicious looking individual—and I had surprising back row company too, a tough swarthy man in a military sort of uniform staring dourly and insisting with a wilful flourish of his hand that I should join him. As I saw a gun at his waist, I did not think I could show unwilling. With my door now shut and our car pulling out rapidly into that busy morning traffic, my captor took out an official pass with his photo and thrust it on display, saying with a surprisingly colloquial command of my idiom, and only a slight Gallic intonation:

"Paul Morrison, if I'm not wrong. Found you at last! I am taking you into custody as it is thought you can probably assist us in looking into a major criminal act. It's to do with an astonishing misappropriation of a quantity of historical gold dug up in a park in South London. I trust you will, (how shall I say?), play ball with us all".

I was dumbstruck and could only concur with a nod. My captor swung forward to prompt our man in front to put his foot down:

"Caporal, vas-y, illico. Au commissariat."

I instantly thought in panic: "What about my job?" How could I warn my work contacts about such a fortuitous AWOL? But it was as if this guardian was tuning into my mind at that instant, by continuing . . .

"You should not worry too much about not turning up for work today. First thing this morning, I told your Ministry collaborators that you cannot go in for a day or so. I simply said that my branch has to obtain your aid as a linguist in a sub-rosa inquiry. This short hiatus should not disturb in any way your ongoing position in that institution. That is, assuming any adjudication you obtain today is strictly 'not guilty'".

"Thank you" was all I could put into words.

As our transport was by now racing southwards into this city's suburbs, my brain was racing in panic, puzzling as to what approach I should adopt in any discussion of my marginal part in that prodigious coup. But mindful that I was in no way a guilty participant, in truth I ought not to worry too much. Should anybody ask what I know about Dimitri's vanishing act, I would simply impart what scant information I had from him in his various mails. In fact, I frankly thought it doubtful that anything I might say would assist much in locating him by now. Apart from that, I was wishing I could contact my confidant Doctor Smith and ask him for handy tips on managing any grilling through which I was put. But I was on my own now.

With no significant holdups, our car was soon crossing on top of Paris's notoriously busy ring road (groaning with stationary traffic as usual) and was racing southwards.

As I was still in shock and showing no opposition to my kidnap, my guardian's mood took a comforting turn. Smiling now and inclining my way, this official said: "I fancy that I find you puzzling about our port of call this morning. It's our commissariat in Orly airport. That's right, way out of town and harm's way. And far from any prying looks from paparazzi and TV or radio hacks, or from crooks in particular.

"This is a highly hush-hush inquiry, involving fact-finding missions coming in, not just from this country of ours or Britain but from around our world. It aims to bring to light, halt and punish an alarming burst of criminality apropos of purloining and trafficking in a vast hoard of costly works of art. It is also looking into rabid corruption among high officialdom—and that ugly word "mafia" is on most folks' lips. Russia is a major culprit in it all but it's particularly rampant in Paris too. In fact, it is now obvious that this shady activity is using our city of light as its world HQ.

"An additional point in favour of Orly is that it allows a constant flow of participants to fly in and out again—judiciously—to input into this tribunal. All that is said in this location must stay untold and unknown. Any publicity at this point could turn out disastrous. So I must insist that "mum is your word". Is that plain?"

"Obviously" was all I could say.

Our transport was by now off that busy motorway south, taking minor roads through Orly town and driving into its airport through a military control point. It took a right turn along a narrow out of bounds approach road, past hangars and aircraft parking bays to stop at an anonymous long squat building. A guard post stood in front with a national tricolour flag flapping on top. As I got out, I got a wink from my custodian who said "good luck" and was away. I was hoping that all my inquisitors this coming day would turn out as convivial.

I was shown into a spacious courtroom and told to sit in a solitary high chair in its midst, waiting in isolation almost half an hour. Finally an imposing group of officials was filing in and sitting down on high chairs on a platform facing my box.

It was a cosmopolitan crowd. A pair of British consular officials, two backroom assistants from Scotland Yard, various MI6, CIA and Russian NVD staff (or should I say FSB or SVR—how was I to know?), hand in hand with a group of local criminal consultants, all sat around a broad circular dais looking my way, with a tall bald chairman in its midst.

With all this commission in situ, its authoritarian adjudicator hit a small brass gong in front of him for our tribunal to start and said to all around: "Good day and *bonjour* to you all. It is most gratifying to find so many of you with us today. My thanks for coming. I trust this will turn out a satisfactory convocation for us. But first, to all in this room, I must insist again that this is not strictly a court of law. It is a fact-finding mission run in total privacy. I say this as our task boils down to obtaining input from individuals having only a minor implication in art traffic, but who might in addition harbour occasional links with mafia organisations.

"Our pact with such folk as you (said looking fractiously my way) is providing you with immunity from adjudication for any information you might hold on any such criminal consortium or activity. That is to say, it's all about catching and absolving minnows to land big fish.

And turning to a row of silk gowns on his right: "You may now start our inquiry. Carry on with our first informant, *s'il vous plaît*".

I had to say who I was and I was told that a suspicion of a major misappropriation of works of art of significant worth was laid at my door. Notwithstanding our chairman's conciliatory affirmation, I was put through a constant antagonistic grilling by a typical old British public school sort of inquisitor, rapt on proving my guilt.

"But your implication in this illicit act is obvious, my man. According to our laboratory analysis, a batch of old gold coins, found in a local church charity box, all had prints of your DNA. And I am told that a match of that DNA has shown up on a lift button and your doorknob in that Parisian Ministry building in which you work. Your guilt is obvious. How can you possibly contradict such a finding?"

I could not do so, calling to mind with horror Doctor Smith's warning about my foolhardy disposal of such booty in that church trunk. But I did my utmost to claim that I was constantly trying to avoid any wilful implication in that criminal act. That handful of coins was an unsought parting gift from my companion who ran away with his haul, and my wish was to unload that trivial portion as soon as I could. A snort of disdain was my inquisitor's backlash.

A taciturn Parisian official sitting on his right was starting to murmur to him. Turning back again my way, my assailant was now fully wound up.

"This worthy functionary on my right is anxious to know how you got into this country. His staff has found no proof, via passport scrutiny or CCTV, of you passing through any immigration control point."

Now I had to start lying, which I was not good at doing. I obviously did not wish to talk about Doctor Smith's participation in my flight. So I told that judicial body about my vocal shortcoming and how I had had an invitation to work in Paris with Oulipo, an organisation caring for individuals who display similar symptoms. For transport, my option (taking my financial hardship into account) was hitchhiking to Ashford, boarding a train across to Calais and thumbing lifts down to Paris—all of which I did without coming across any passport controls.

Both had a short mumbling discussion, following which my assailant did a nod towards his chairman, who said I should now stand down but stay in that courtroom to await any additional probing.

A factotum in uniform at that point slid warily into our room to murmur to that adjudicator, who was soon nodding and smiling at what was obviously surprising but important input.

"I am told that a significant participant in criminal activity with assiduous links to our art world and who is right on top of our priority list for today has just flown in. Bring him in straight away for quizzing"

A buzz ran around our throng. A back door was quickly ajar and a familiar individual was slowly walking in . . . It was Dimitri.

My worthy companion, with a stubbly chin and sporting an ill-fitting khaki uniform was looking haggard and thoroughly downcast. Such a contrast in my mind with that vibrant runaway I last saw scaling that back wall with his box of bullion. Dimitri was glancing suspiciously around that broad courtroom panorama. But on his finally looking my way, I saw an instant transformation in him. From a scowl to a broad grin and a rapid wink of affinity. At last I had convivial company!

His particular inquisitor was also draconian but Dimitri was showing an amazing ability at first in handling a razor-sharp inquisition and lying in a most convincing way. My companion was claiming that his plan all along was to transport that gold straightaway to a Swiss bank, strictly so that it did not fall into Mafiosi hands, whilst hoping for a thankful bonus from any organisation with a right to own it. But this plot was to miscarry badly. Shortly following his arrival in his Swiss sanctuary, his British paramour put a strong drug into his usual nightcap (a vodka and tonic) which had him out flat and unconscious for a full day and a half. Whilst that cool lady took flight with his total hoard, planning to hand it across to a rival pack of Russian contacts, claiming a quota of that loot.

For this act of charity, as Dimitri was shortly to find out from his own contacts, Barbara was bound in chains and cast away in a small dinghy a long way off Savona (a Ligurian coastal town) by that band of rascals who got going southwards, sailing with that box of numismatic antiquity, in a 40 foot yacht first to Sicily and onwards to Cyprus and to who knows what distant harbour, out of harm's way.

Such was that amazing story which was starting to unfold during that morning. I could only trust that Barbara, also a villain with a plan that would fall apart, was rapidly found and brought back to land unhurt.

Dimitri was initially on top form in monopolising court activity by holding forth for a good half hour with his affidavit and supplying copious misinformation, which had no rapport to any of his doubtful activity and in so doing, was tiring his assailants. But this was not to last till doomsday. His main inquisitor, wiping his damp distraught brow, finally had to stoop for a quick word with a swarthy individual to his right who quickly stood up with a blazing look. It was a man from Moscow.

Straightaway his attack was brutal—and was all said in Russian. Dimitri at first was smiling, thinking this was a sanction for him to talk back flowingly in his own idiom. But as Dimitri was launching into a tall story *po russki*, a strong command rang out from that mission's chairman: "No, *gaspodin*, I'm sorry—but that's totally out of court. Our Russian companion has a right to play his part in his local vocabulary, but you must talk back in our British idiom so that all of us around can follow your affidavit."

From this point on, Dimitri's showing was waning fast and his poor grasp of our idiom was now plain for all to spot. My old companion found it hard to absorb a constant flow of pugnacious grilling and probing and shouting—"Not that fairy story—I want truth!" "*Pravda, tovarisch, pozhalouista!*" And watching Dimitri having to switch rapidly from Russian to our own idiom and back again, I saw damp blobs start rolling down his brow and his flow of words was vacillating to a halt.

In fact with this bullying, Dimitri was by now having nightmarish flashbacks to past painful traumas—brutal brainwashing by Party manipulators, occurring in his distant childhood, following a roundup of all his family which was wrongly put into custody for committing acts of spying for capitalism. Dimitri was again a lost young boy, solo, in a dark room with a strong shaft of light blinding him and a background sound of aquatic dripping or bloodcurdling howls torturing him.

Giving in at last to his assailant's accusations, Dimitri could only sob and admit to gross misconduct and to a host of accusations, laid at his door. His assailant was now smiling and was handing back to his chairman.

A ruling on our lot was quick in coming. My Russian collaborator was to stay in custody and to assist his guardians in unmasking that labyrinth of his country's mafia organisations. With a sycophantic "thank you", I was found not guilty of any misdoing, nor of any worth in supplying data on any shady activity but simply told that I should just carry on with my job in Paris.

As Dimitri was shown out by two guards, my pal, unsurprisingly in fact, was to turn my way, transmit a mutinous wink and hold up a fist of insubordination, making it obvious that his sorrowful final conduct in court was, in part, play-acting. Thus I could count on Dimitri finding a wily and victorious way out *à la fin*. But sadly I was not to run into him again.

This curious convocation was now standing up and withdrawing from this courtroom, gossiping about our input without looking my way, whilst I sat puzzling what might occur from now onwards. Nobody said I could or should withdraw and so I stood (or sat) my ground on my own. With this vast room now void, I was growing cross and thinking about storming out (although I was puzzling as to how I might hitch a lift back to Paris).

But through a back door in that courtroom, amazingly, I saw a familiar individual striding my way, showing a broad grin. It was Doctor Smith, in body and soul. I sat down in shock.

"It's such a tonic to run into you again, Paul. I am bid by this organisation to thank you for your contribution to this curious mission. Your "not guilty" status was not in doubt at any point, but it was obligatory for us all to put you through today's grilling to confirm it".

I was dumbstruck. What was my old doctor, guru and confidant doing, taking part in this hush-hush mission, lost in a Parisian airport, acting as if an important part of its staff? I had had constant contact with him via my PC, providing tidings about my various sorts of Oulipo activity and as I did so, I normally had in my mind a vision of him in his study in sunny Slough. But to find him now, acting a major part in this incognito inquiry? Absurd!

"You and I must do a lot of catching up, don't you think?" my doctor was continuing. "But I am still busy right now. My car is in front of this building. If that's all right with you, I'll ask my man to run you back straightaway to your flat in Paris.

"A final thought. As you just had to go through such a grim day, my proposal is for both of us to wind down and chat tonight in a first class culinary institution. That's what Paris is all about, don't you think? And it's my invitation, Paul, I insist. It is known as Apicius. It has two stars, and its food is out of this world. Its *patron* is a magician with mushrooms, a virtuoso with fish, such as bass, prawns and all sorts of aquatic arthropods. To its patrons, it's known as 'truth cooking'. To my mind, it's ambrosia.

"So if it's all right with you, I'll pick you up tonight at half six. Is that OK?"

With such a glorious finish to such a worrying day, what could I say but "thanks a million"?

XXIII

Following a short obligatory nap and a long hot bath back in my flat, I was fighting fit again and looking forward not only to our forthcoming tuck-in, but in particular to finding out what my host for this night was up to in collaboration with that global band of criminologists I saw today. Doctor Smith was still in bright spirits on arriving to transport us both to Apicius. (His right hand man usually driving his car had a night off). It was a short run as traffic was surprisingly light, with him asking how my work at my Ministry in Paris was going and how much living in this city was to my liking. Arriving at Apicius, a smiling host, conscious of Doc's status as a habitual visitor, warmly bid us *bonsoir* and took our car away for parking.

In a first class position in a spacious and stylish ground floor salon in this small mansion, with its rich colourful floral displays all around, both of us sat looking up at an array of futuristic art. A glass of bubbly was rapidly brought in for us to drink a toast to our common good physical condition, as Doctor Smith was starting to clarify his implication in that day's grand inquiry.

"It's all fairly logical if you think about it. As you know, my activity is assisting anybody with any sort of communication block, such as your infirmity, which is not uncommon. Our study of long-lasting vocal invalids and all our work with ongoing Oulipo workshops on a global basis has shown that anybody with this handicap usually also has, as a consolation, distinct inborn analytical and psychic gifts. In particular, an ability for formulating and handling coding and cryptograms—and so can do important work for MI6, or similar organisations. You will find that many a happy pupil in your Paris class, is working for DCRI or SCSSI as a spy, to put it bluntly, and just abandons that daily occult activity for an hour or so to sit in on your class. That common ground shows why I maintain constant links with multinational anti-criminal missions such as that on which you sat today. Our shady worlds of spying, criminology and psycholinguistics must finally all work in harmony.

"At which point I must now turn to your Ministry job. So far, I am told your showing is highly thought of. Bravo, I am glad for you. But just think for an instant how virtually all that group of officials in that diplomatic building, whom you coach in talking and writing lipogrammatically, will also fit into that cloak and poniard classification".

Doctor Smith and I had now to abstain from this gossip to focus on such outstanding gastronomic options, now laid out on display in front of us—roast turbot and lamb on a spit. Small talk was to follow as both of us sank into that warm mood of satisfaction coming from such outstanding food and *grands vins fins*. Whilst my host was cautious with his thirst, no doubt on account of driving back, I was savouring such *crus* with brio, finally sampling a glass of Raymond Ragnaud Cognac XO as a worthy swan song to a significant night out.

Withdrawing blissfully not far short of midnight from that sanctuary of high living, my brain was languishing. But to my host's inquiry about my ongoing plans, I did confirm that I was totally in favour of inhabiting *ad finitum* this stimulating City of Light, doing my Ministry job or going back to running my Oulipo class. I was on top form.

For all that, on arriving back in his car in front of my flat, Doctor Smith was to disturb my warm tranquillity with parting tidings of such import that I would abruptly find that I would not, in a month of Sundays, succumb to any placid dormancy that coming night.

"Prior to bidding you a good long nap, Paul, I must just bring up a final ticklish topic. It's about Lisa". My spirits sank.

"Your paramour got in touch last Monday without warning and was in a sad humour. Lisa was wanting first of all to book a consultation at my hospital for a communication diagnosis. That was intriguing. But also to ask how to go about locating you. I thought I ought not to supply any particular information about your situation without consulting you first. I was obviously cautious, but finally I did grant that I would transmit this bit of mail on any occasion at which I was in contact with you. Don't look at it straightaway. I fancy it's for you to go through and absorb on your own, up in your flat."

I was in such shock that I did not think to say 'thank you', as Doctor Smith, smiling kindly now, was continuing: "Apart from this abrupt jog from your past, my parting wish is for you to carry on, now and again, forwarding my way a summary of all your activity. It's important for both of us to stay in touch. You look on good form. Stay that way. And bravo for your handling of this morning's grilling. You put on a convincing show. You can put it all out of your mind now. And tonight was most convivial—you and I should do it again soon". And with that and a knowing wink, my good doctor was driving off rapidly.

For half an hour, I lay flat on my divan in a dim light, just gazing at that disturbing pink scrap of post I had thrown intact onto my pillow. I found it hard to summon up any motivation to find out what it was all about. But in my gut I had to admit that I did still harbour a soft spot for that lady's soft spots. Finally I slit its back to look at what it said. It was such a body blow. Winning back Lisa's favours was by now absurd.

I just cannot say out loud to you or any mortal what was said in that short dispatch. In no way could any of what Lisa had to put into words find its way into my mouth or into this story. In fact, it is obvious that I am now simply "Jack Sprat who could swallow no fat". And Lisa would find it taboo to tuck into sirloin or rump.

So I must sadly bid you "so long" at this point and thank you for following this publication of my Calvary. I will allow you to find out all about my plight, by just glancing at this codicil which follows.

That is if Doctor Smith should go on to publish this rambling composition . . . .

Strictly for

Paul

By Hand

Dearest friend

These few lines discover me very distressed—indeed overwrought. The five weeks since we parted have been the longest saddest time ever. Those afternoons we enjoyed entertaining ourselves, then those passionate evenings getting merry together, embracing each other, seem presently like unreal remote dreams.

Humble apologies re unsympathetic behaviour are therefore required. They are sincerely expressed herein. Give me hope. Please forgive me. Strange mental problems, serious speaking difficulties needing some explanation have suddenly begun affecting me. They are quite frightening, leaving me wondering whether they resemble those verbal defects affecting yourself.

Fondest love
ME
Elisa

Please note: Previous brief signature impossible. Have necessarily added another letter, reusing after countless years the complete name received when christened. Everything's suddenly gone haywire!

Let's meet sometime next week! Make me euphoric—telephone me immediately—same number!

POSTSCRIPT

A word about Lipograms and Oulipo

Art in all its many forms springs from inspiration and originality, but also from constraint. And constraint is what this book is all about: though in approach it is not particularly original.

This story is what is known as a lipogram (a composition in which you constantly avoid using words containing a particular sign of our abc).

My introduction into this absurd lipogrammatical world was a random find, many moons ago in a Paris bookshop, of that highly original magnum opus—*La Disparition*. From start to finish this most amusing work shuns abc's fifth symbol (that small partially round animal with a broad grin) throughout. No such sign is found so constantly in vocabulary in many idioms around our world. Pull out any book in that Gallic idiom and count just how many occasions you find it in print.

By and by, I also found out about a book (from way back) with a similar limitation using my own British vocabulary—*Gadsby*—and also *A Void*, a translation by G. Adair of *La Disparition.* From all this scrutiny, I got wind of a multinational artistic organisation known as Oulipo, which fashions and champions such distinct forms of communication. (For full information, look it up on Wiki or visit Oulipo on www!)

As this taboo symbol is not found in my full ID as shown in my passport, it did cross my mind that this was a substantial prompt to look into writing my own "Oulipo" book in my own idiom following this taxing constraint—and making Oulipo part of its plot. A daunting task but not as arduous, I think, as a composition in Balzac's or Proust's or Camus' patois. My plan was to avoid (sorry for that pun!) any contact with any lipogrammatical works in my idiom that you can buy today until my own absurd story had got to its conclusion—and into print. It has—and I trust that you find it amusing to spot its constant substitution of synonyms.

You may ask why I allow my vocabulary in this opus to contain groups of initials (such as AWOL, HQ, ID, TV and so forth) which stand for word groups that, in full, actually contain our rascal. I do so only if pronouncing such initials is customary.

To that grand Oulipopulation in Paris and throughout our world, my gracious salutations!